"Shelby!" Teresa called firmly. "Go Mark!"

Her voice was loud and clear. The lizard raced up a skinny tree trunk, out of my reach, as I turned my head to look at Teresa.

She was looking at me intently. I looked back. Was there something she wanted?

A smell drifted toward me from the table. Yes! A treat was lying on it. Even better than a lizard! I ran toward the table, jumped up to put my front feet on its surface, and snapped up the treat.

"Shelby, good girl. Good girl," Teresa praised.

I loved her voice when she told me I was a good girl. It was almost as marvelous as a treat.

Also by
W. Bruce Cameron

Shelby's Story

A Dog's Way Home Tale

W. Bruce Cameron

Illustrations by
Richard Cowdrey

STARSCAPE

A Tom Doherty Associates Book
New York

SHELBY'S STORY

Copyright © 2018 by W. Bruce Cameron

Reading and Activity Guide copyright © 2018 by Tor Books

Illustrations © 2018 by Richard Cowdrey

All rights reserved.

A Starscape Book
Published by Tom Doherty Associates
120 Broadway
New York, NY 10271

www.tor-forge.com

The Library of Congress has cataloged the hardcover edition as follows:

Cameron, W. Bruce, author.
 Shelby's story : a dog's way home tale / W. Bruce Cameron ; illustrations by
Richard Cowdrey.—First edition.
  p. cm.
"A Tom Doherty Associates book."
 ISBN 978-1-250-30191-8 (hardcover)
 ISBN 978-1-250-30192-5 (ebook)
1. Rescue dogs—Fiction. 2. Working dogs—Fiction. 3. Dogs—Fiction. 4. Human-
animal relationships—Fiction. I. Title.
 PZ7.C1442 Sh 2018
 [Fic]—dc23

2018040319

ISBN 978-1-250-81442-5 (Costco edition)

Our books may be purchased in bulk for promotional, educational, or business use.
Please contact your local bookseller or the Macmillan Corporate and Premium
Sales Department at 1-800-221-7945, extension 5442, or by email
at MacmillanSpecialMarkets@macmillan.com.

First Edition: November 2018
First Costco Edition: April 2021

Printed in the United States of America

0 9 8 7 6 5 4 3 2 1

For Teresa A. Miller, Thomas "TJ" Jordi,
Megan Buhler, Brian Turi,
and April Morley:
Thank you for helping Shelby be
loved, safe, happy, and warm.

Shelby's Story

A Dog's Way Home Tale

1

There are just a few things I can remember about my earliest days.

Of course, there was my mother. At first I could not see her, but I could smell her and feel the comforting heat of her body beneath her thick fur. My mother was warmth and safety and milk that filled my stomach and left me sleepy and content, curled up next to her.

I could hear noises, too. Sometimes there were sharp yips or squeaks. Sometimes a bang that made me twitch, even in my dreams. There was a rattling, clanking sound that I heard regularly, and a little trickling noise that never went away.

I found it all so soothing. The trickling sound, my

mother, and the comfort of furry bodies sleeping close together.

That was how everything started.

After a few days, my eyes opened and I was able to stay awake longer than before. I began to learn things.

I learned that my mother was big and short-haired and white, with a wet nose and a wide, blocky face. Her tongue was long, and strong enough that when she washed me with it I fell over.

I had brothers and a sister, too! That came as something of a surprise. They were the source of the little yips and squeals that I heard. They were part of what kept me warm, too, so I liked them, even if they did step on me quite a lot.

Two of my brothers were white, just like my mother. Another was brown, black, and white in patches. My sister was brown and black with a tiny splotch of white on her chest—just like me. In my mind, I named her Splotch.

The trickling noise that I heard night and day came from a long, twisty hose that lay on the ground. Water ran out of this, dripping into a metal bowl. Sometimes my mother went over to take a drink from the bowl. I didn't bother, though, and neither did my littermates. Milk from our mother was all we needed.

The bang that I heard so often came, I discovered, from a house nearby. Twice a day, a door in that house would open and a person would come down a few steps into the yard where we lived.

The door would slam shut behind her with a sharp, loud sound and the person would shuffle forward. She'd put a bowl full of brown stuff down on the ground near our mother and then return inside the house.

She was the first human I'd ever seen. Frankly, I didn't think she was very interesting. She never stayed to talk to us or pet us, so I decided she was not someone I had to care much about.

When she put the bowl down on the ground, my mother would get up, sometimes shaking off a puppy or two, and walk over to it. Then I would hear that clanking sound once again. It came from the chain that was attached to my mother's collar. The other end of that chain was connected to a long stake driven into the ground.

When my mother moved, the chain clanked. When she shook her head or stretched, the chain rang with a harsh music. When she settled down again, the chain was quiet.

My mother would put her nose in the bowl and gobble up the brown stuff inside. When my legs grew a bit stronger, I sometimes went over to sniff at it, but it never smelled very exciting to me. I didn't see why my mother liked it so much.

There were lots of other things in the yard that were

more interesting than a bowl full of brown chunks. As I got older, I was able to learn more about them.

Dandelions, for one. They were fuzzy yellow circles attached to strong stems. They did not taste very good, but when I bit at them they bobbed and danced on their stems, and that was almost like a game.

Sticks, too! Sticks were everywhere. And sticks *did* taste good, especially as my teeth started to come in and I could gnaw off bits of bark.

The other good thing about sticks was that my brothers and sister wanted them' too. That meant, if I had a stick and they didn't, it was time for a game called I've-Got-the-Stick-and-You-Don't.

I *loved* that game!

My sister was especially good at playing it. My brothers wanted to remain closer to my mother's side, but if I had a stick Splotch would chase me until I dropped it and she could snatch it. Then it was my turn to chase her.

What a marvelous thing to do!

Day by day, Splotch and I grew stronger, and our play took us all over the yard. We played other things too. There was Chase-Me and I'm-the-One-On-Top and Look-How-Fierce-I-Can-Be. All of them were delightful games, and after we were done we'd run back to my mother for a meal of milk and a good long sleep.

This was my life until the day the door banged open and the human lady put down a bowl for my mother and also a tray full of dark-colored goop. My brothers and Splotch and I *loved* that stuff! We licked it and chewed it and stood in it and rolled in it. I ate it from the tray and my feet and Splotch's face. Glop was the best! I still went to my mother to nurse, but more for comfort than hunger, now that my siblings were covered with glop and I could snack anytime I wanted!

One day after I'd licked Splotch's face clean of glop and she'd licked mine, we began to wrestle. Splotch shook me off, and I rolled and kept rolling until I bumped up against something I'd seen but never thought much about.

The fence.

It was the first time I'd really examined the fence. It went all the way around our yard, and it was made of chilly wire that did not taste good. I know, because I tried to bite it.

Splotch came over and chewed on my ear, trying to get my attention. But I shook my head so that she fell over, and kept sniffing at the fence.

Something had caught my attention.

On the other side of the fence I could detect a new smell. And it was very, very interesting.

Later I would find out that the smell I'd encountered here, for the first time, was called a piece of chicken.

I didn't know that then. All I knew was that my tail began springing back and forth even faster than my nose was twitching.

I was growing fast in those days, and my brothers and sister were, too. I ate as much glop as I could before it was all gone, but I was still a little hungry all the time.

The brown stuff in my mother's bowl was starting to smell interesting to me. And this thing on the other side of the fence smelled a little like the chunks in that bowl . . . but better. Much, much better. So much better that I licked my lips.

I put my nose down to the spot where the fence met the ground and sniffed harder. The delicious new smell was so close . . . only a few inches away. But the fence kept my nose from reaching it.

Splotch had figured out what I was doing. She came to the fence and put her nose right next to mine. She sniffed hard as well.

I pushed at her nose, she pushed at mine, and we discovered something extraordinary.

A hole!

The fence had a gap in it, right where the metal wire met the ground. It was not a large hole. My mother would never have been able to fit through it. But when I lay down flat on my tummy and wiggled and pushed with my back feet, I could shove myself through it.

Now I was on the other side of the fence. And the thing that smelled so good was right next to me on the ground!

I grabbed at it, but it slipped out of my teeth. Splotch had wiggled through the fence behind me and she grabbed at the treat as well, but the same thing happened to her. We were not used to chewing yet, and our jaws were not strong.

But we didn't give up. We both nibbled and licked at that piece of chicken, and after a few more tries we each ripped off a tiny mouthful that tasted marvelous. I gulped and it slid right down my throat into my stomach, and that made me anxious for more.

In a few minutes the chicken was entirely gone and my sister and I were both licking at the greasy spot on the grass where it had lain.

From inside the yard, I heard a sharp, urgent bark. It was our mother. I looked up and saw her standing as close to the fence as her chain would let her get. She barked again, and I understood.

I wiggled back under the fence, with Splotch following, and ran up to my mother, tail wagging, trying to tell her what a wonderful adventure I'd had. She sniffed me all over and did the same to my sister, and then she nudged me until I lay down with her.

I had a good sleep, close to my mother and littermates. But I didn't forget what I'd found on the other side of the fence.

That bit of wonderful food stayed on my mind as my brothers and sister and I continued to grow. My mother stopped nursing us, turning away from the sharp little teeth we'd all sprouted. Which meant I was on glop-only. Which should have been fine except there never seemed to be enough! I always wanted more. When I curled up to sleep at night, my stomach sometimes growled as if it were angry at me.

That hole in the fence drew me back time and time again. Was there more food outside? More of that wonderful piece of chicken? Maybe even something . . . better?

Better than chicken? I drooled at the thought. I *dreamed* about it.

I would lean against the fence and sniff. Once I even squirmed through. But there was no more chicken on the ground, and I couldn't smell any nearby. Or anything else to eat.

My mother barked a warning, and I wiggled back through the fence to cuddle close to her and be licked and sniffed.

But my stomach growled loudly at me that night. It wanted to be fed.

The next day, I returned to the hole in the fence.

Splotch came with me. I put my head into the hole and sniffed, while my sister tried to climb on my back.

I didn't smell more chicken. But I smelled . . . something.

It was a *big* smell. That was the only way I could describe it to myself. It combined dirt and grass and water and small furry animals that moved quickly. Included in this smell were other dogs and people and dust and wind and harsh, smoky odors that came from the cars that went up and down the street near our yard.

It was the smell of the world outside our yard. And that world must have more food in it. Somewhere in that world there would be another piece of chicken. Or maybe just more glop.

I did not want to leave my mother. Part of me wanted to stay in the yard, playing and wrestling with my littermates, sleeping close to my family's warmth.

But the smell of the world called to me. It seemed to pull me through the hole in the fence.

Splotch fell off my back, and I wiggled and pushed with my back legs. The hole seemed to have gotten smaller since the first time I tried it, which was strange. It was a tight fit, but I still managed to squeeze through.

Splotch followed me.

I looked back and saw my mother sitting where she always sat, attached by the chain to the stake in the ground. She tilted her head and watched me. But this time she did not bark to call me back.

Maybe she knew about the world and how big it smelled, even if she could not go with us. She could not fit through the hole, and her chain kept her in one place.

But I thought she might understand about the chicken. I thought she knew it was time for Splotch and me to find it. Or whatever else there might be.

2

My sister and I began to learn about the world very quickly. One of the first things we learned was that the world was full of wheels and that dogs need to stay away from them.

Once we squeezed through the fence, we wandered along a narrow space with our metal fence on one side and a different, wooden fence on the other. This took us to something new—a hard path set into the grass. It ran farther out into the world than we could see, and I could smell that many, many different feet had walked upon it.

I had my nose down, sniffing hard, when something rushed past me, much faster than any puppy could run.

There were two round black things—wheels—spinning very quickly, and a person riding on top of the wheels.

"Watch out, puppy!" this person yelled as he spun past.

I leaped back with a startled yelp. Splotch sat down and yipped at the strange thing that had hurried by.

I didn't like it. Wheels, I decided, were not kind to dogs.

Other things hurried past on wheels as well. These were cars. I knew about them, because I could see and hear and smell them from our yard. They went even faster than the thing with two wheels. But sometimes they stopped and didn't move at all.

It was confusing.

One of these cars stopped close to us, and that's when I realized that they were something like metal boxes on wheels. Inside the boxes were people! I figured that out because a door in the box opened and someone came out.

This person was smaller than the woman who brought food in the metal bowls. "Oh, Mommy! Puppies!" she called out in a high voice.

"Samantha, get back inside," another voice answered.

"But Mommy . . . ," the small person said. She came toward us with her hand out.

She smelled interesting—sweet and soapy. But she'd just gotten out of the thing with wheels and I did not like wheels.

I ran away. My sister followed.

"Awww. . . . ," said the small person sadly.

"I'm sure they live around here. They're probably headed home right now," said the other voice. "Come on, Samantha, back in the car. We're going to be late."

The thing with wheels rushed away.

Things with wheels! People of different sizes! I wondered what else I'd find out here in the world.

Food, it turned out. I'd been right when I thought that there was going to be food beyond the fence.

So many different kinds of food!

I saw that Splotch, ahead of me, was sniffing at a big plastic bag sitting next to our hard path. She seemed excited about it, so I rushed up to see what was so interesting.

Inside the plastic, there was definitely food. I could smell it!

My sister bit at the plastic. I did the same. She gripped with her teeth and shook her head. I tightened up my jaws as well, and when she pulled at the plastic I yanked the other way.

It ripped.

What fell out onto the grass was amazing. There was a big lump of mushy meat. There were bits of bread in another plastic bag that my sister quickly tore to shreds. There was a paper carton with a little milk sloshing inside it. That was hard to chew open, but I did and managed to lick up some of the milk before it drained away into the grass.

How wonderful! We'd been right to come through the fence.

"Hey, get out of that!" somebody yelled. "Get away from there!"

I didn't look up. I was busy getting the last of the milk.

"Move it!" the voice shouted. Now it was louder.

Then a rock fell out of the air right next to my nose. I jumped back, shaking my head. Milk droplets scattered.

The next rock hit me right on my rump!

It stung. I spun around with a surprised yelp and saw a person coming toward us. His face and his shoulders and his stride looked angry. He had another rock in his hand, and he drew it back, ready to throw.

This was like the wheels, I realized. It was a danger. The world had amazing food, but it also held dangers for dogs. The best thing to do with danger was to run away from it.

I did. Splotch stayed close to me and we raced off down the hard path, farther and farther away from the yard with the hole in the fence where our mother and brothers were.

"Look at this mess!" the person with the rock called behind us. "I'm going to be late to work now. Stupid dogs! Stay away if you know what's good for you!"

My sister and I ran until we came to a corner. We turned it so that we'd be out of the sight of the angry man with the rocks. There was a bush growing next to the hard path, and we huddled under it, close together.

I licked my sister's muzzle, which still had a little bit of that mushy meat clinging to it.

We were both tired, so we slept there together. When I woke, it was dark.

I knew about darkness. It became dark every night in our yard, and sometimes a little cold. The thing to do with darkness was to cuddle close to someone warm and wait for it to go away.

My sister was not as warm as my mother. Still, I squirmed close to her, and she did the same thing to me. We stayed under our bush until the light came back, and then I discovered that my stomach was empty again.

Stomachs are a lot of work.

My sister and I crawled out from under our bush, ready to find another plastic bag full of food. To our surprise, there were none! We looked up and down the hard path, but we didn't see a single plastic bag anywhere.

I wondered if we should try to make our way back

to the yard and find our mother and brothers. There would be that tray of glop there. Even if it wasn't enough, it would be something.

But I wasn't quite sure which way to go to find the yard again, and Splotch had already wandered a little way down the hard path. She found a new yard where a metal contraption was spraying water all over. Fun!

She barked and jumped at the flying water, and I joined her for a bit. Then I lapped up a drink from a puddle. It did not fill up my belly like the meat and milk from yesterday, but it helped.

Now, food. This was the world, and it should have some food in it. We'd already found chicken here, and meat, and bread, and milk. We'd find something else. I was sure of it.

And this turned out to be true. But it was more work than I'd expected. We walked and walked. The hard path ended, houses became much more spread apart, and the road went from being smooth to having holes and ruts and gravel and dirt. We were so far from Mother, now, that I could almost feel her worrying about us. I think Splotch and I both were ready to turn back, but time and time again the smell of food would lure us on.

Sometimes the food that we found was a bit of paper or cardboard with a little meat or sauce smeared on it. Sometimes it was a crinkly bag with crumbs of something salty inside. Sometimes it was a plastic cup with sweet drops sticking to its sides.

Every now and then a person would come out of a house to shout something at us, and then we'd run away. More rarely, someone would speak gently to us and maybe toss some food on the ground—a piece of bread with cheese and tomato, or a scrap of meat with tangy sauce.

Splotch and I inched closer to grab the food and then darted away to safety to eat it. We had been learning that people were not to be trusted, not even if they gave us something to eat. You never knew when they might shout or throw rocks.

We were *hungry*. I loved Splotch and the only way I could keep my mind off my hunger was to play with her, but we both seemed to tire very quickly.

Some days we found almost enough to quiet our bellies and let us sleep in peace. Some days we did not.

The best days were the ones in which we found a large plastic container. They were marvelous!

Inside them I could smell all *sorts* of things. Meaty, cheesy, spicy, sweet, greasy, fabulous smells. Smells that made my tail wag wildly and drool drip down from my muzzle to the ground.

The trouble was that the smells were *inside* and my sister and I were *outside*. That was frustrating, and the opposite of how we wanted things to be.

The big bins had lids, but sometimes plastic bags full of delicious smells were piled high, forcing the lids open. Splotch and I would try to climb up to snatch the bags at the top of the heap, usually stepping on each other. As irritating as it could be to have Splotch's paw on my face, I forgave her if she fell back, pulling a bag with her. We were experts now in tearing open the plastic to get at the morsels of food within.

The best was when there would be a bag on the dirt next to the bin. We'd rip into that in an instant. Then we'd dig into all the treasures that poured out. After a while a human would usually come running over and yell at us, and then we'd take off. But our stomachs would be full, at least for a little while.

When darkness came, we'd sleep under bushes or near cars with missing doors and the clear smell of neglect mingled with the vines twisting through the rotting seats. We were warm enough if we curled up together, except when it rained.

I did *not* like rain.

I remembered it from the yard, tiny bits of water falling from the sky. I hadn't minded it so much then, because I could curl up with my mother, pushing deep into her fur, and stay warm even if I was wet.

But when it rained on my sister and me, we got cold. Always. We just weren't big enough to keep each other warm. There was nothing we could do, however, but wait and shiver until the rain stopped and the light re-turned.

Then we'd go back to work filling our bellies. It was hard. But we didn't know anything else to do.

My sister and I had lived out in the world for quite a while when something happened that showed how right we had been to stay away from people.

Splotch and I had seized a plastic bag from a container and torn it open. I had my head inside it, trying to reach a particularly succulent bit of flat bread soaked in sweet, sticky sauce when I heard my sister bark sharply.

I pulled my head out and turned around. A small truck had pulled up next to the container, and a man and a woman had gotten out. They were walking slowly toward us. The woman had a long stick in her hand.

"These look like the dogs we've gotten so many calls about," the man said. "Hey there. Don't worry, now. We're here to help."

I backed up, even though my stomach was empty and it was hard to leave the bag with all its enticing smells. Splotch backed away, too.

But we had our eyes on the man who was talking to

us, and we'd forgotten to watch the woman with the stick. She had moved quietly around behind us, so we were backing up right toward her!

Splotch yelped in panic, and I spun around to see that the woman had lowered her stick until one end was near my sister's face. On that end of the stick was a loop of wire, and she slipped that wire right over Splotch's neck!

Splotch was crying and twisting as she tried to get loose. The woman was talking to her gently, but the gentleness of her words did not make the stick any less terrifying.

"Get the other one, Tom!" she called out.

Hands in thick gloves were reaching out toward me. I dodged away. The man stumbled, falling down on one knee.

Splotch was still flinging herself wildly from side to side. "There, there, don't worry, sweetie; it's going to be better soon," the woman told her, but I didn't understand her words. All I knew was that Splotch was frightened and that the loop around her neck was hurting her. I wanted to run to her side and help, bite at that wire loop and make it go away.

But I didn't. I couldn't. Even stronger than the urge to help my sister was another feeling inside me—a feeling that told me to run as far and as fast as I could.

The man grabbed at me again, and I darted to one

side. I yipped once to let my sister know that I was sorry, but I had to go.

Then I ran. I heard heavy footsteps beside me, but I'd had a lot of practice at running. The man could not keep up with me. I dodged beneath a bush and raced into the woods. By then no one was chasing me anymore, but I ran anyway, until I was out of breath.

I never saw my sister again after that. And I tried harder than ever to stay away from people. Even though they sometimes had food, it was not worth getting near them.

It was colder at night without Splotch to sleep beside me, especially when it rained. And I could not pull the bags out of the bins by myself. My stomach became more and more demanding. It felt as if it were clawing at my insides. It made me a little angry. Keeping my stomach filled was such a big job that it took all of my time, and it *still* wasn't satisfied!

I kept an eye out for more of those plastic bags. They were the best source of food I had found yet. They were not there every day, or even most days. When they were, though, I could count on a full belly.

The next time the plastic bags showed up beside the road, I was happy, especially since there were so many, all piled up around a bin with a lid. I was eagerly tearing one open when a big truck pulled up right next to me. Men jumped down from the truck, and I quickly darted away.

To my surprise, the men picked up the bag and flung it into the back of the truck. So many rich, thick, powerful smells came pouring out of that truck! They made my head spin. I backed off farther and watched the men heave up the bin and dump its contents into the truck before jumping back on.

The plastic bags had gone into the truck. I thought about that hard, and I stared after the wonderfully smelly truck as it rumbled slowly away.

Those bags were full of food. That meant the truck was full of food.

That meant it was a good truck, even if it did have people on it. And wheels.

The truck headed steadily down the road. I followed it.

3

I followed the truck a long, long way.

It did not go very fast, and it stopped often. I didn't get too close, in case the men came at me and tried to grab me or to snag my neck in one of those long sticks. I didn't need to keep the truck in sight, because even when it pulled away I could easily track the strong odors trailing after it.

After a while there were almost no houses on the road and the truck didn't make as many stops. I knew it was speeding away from me, but I was too hungry to gallop after it. I just followed my nose.

My stomach was pretending to be a dog, growling at me from within. If it were a dog I would snarl back—I was doing the best I could!

The smell led me down a long, narrow road. I stayed to the side as a car swept past me—wheels! I trotted along a muddy road that felt soft and comfortable to my feet. There were trees on either side of the road, and no houses or buildings at all.

There was noise, though. Up ahead I could hear the growling noise made by trucks. It sounded like my stomach! I could also hear some crashing and banging and occasionally shouts.

The sounds told me to go cautiously. The smell, though . . . , the smell was so enticing that I simply could not stop. There was food up there! It was buried under other scents—rubber, something burning, plastic, the foul smoke from the truck . . . but it was there.

My goal was to get my stomach to shut up and stop growling, so I followed the food smell.

I crept through an open gate in a tall fence, and just up ahead I saw something wonderful.

Plastic bags. Lots of them. A *mountain* of them.

The truck I had followed was stopped, the men watching as the back of it tipped, dumping bags out onto the ground in a huge pile. There were other piles, too. Many, many piles.

My stomach demanded that I rush forward and grab the nearest bag, but I didn't. Instead, I lay down in a clump of tall grass by the roadside and watched. I needed to make sure it was safe before I did anything.

I did not like the truck. It was loud and noisy and belching out that foul-smelling smoke. The people who had taken my sister away from me had gotten out of a truck. I had to stay away from trucks.

My stomach growled again.

There was a pile of plastic bags not far away. Did I dare dash out from my hiding place and grab one? I was afraid.

Then the truck moved on in that jerky way, so different from how dogs and other animals move.

No other trucks were nearby, so that pile of plastic bags was free for the taking.

Some birds seemed to think so, too. They were soaring overhead and beginning to swoop down low toward the bags. Some of them had even ripped a few bags open already. Less work for me!

I darted out, sniffing hard, letting my nose guide me. There were so many smells it was hard to know where to look first! But a salty, greasy, meaty odor grabbed my attention, and I stuck my muzzle into an open bag and snatched at a chunk of chicken, just as delicious as the one Splotch and I had found the first time we'd ventured outside the fence.

Then something in a roll of paper grabbed my attention. I seized it. I knew it! What a wonderful world, with chicken and all sorts of other food laid out for deserving dogs with angry stomachs! This was where

Splotch and I had been heading all along, even though we hadn't known it at the time. If only she were still here!

The rumble of an approaching truck grew louder. My stomach told me to stay and find more and more and more to eat, but my feet told me to run. I dashed back to the clump of grass and ripped the paper open. There was meat inside! It was different from the chicken—crumbled beef and cheese and a sauce—and had a hot taste that burned my mouth, but I was too hungry to care. I gulped it down.

The birds and I were not the only ones interested in the plastic bags and the amazing smells. I looked up from licking the grease off the paper to see a small animal watching me from a pile of dirt nearby.

It was not a dog—it was smaller, and it had slick fur and tiny triangular ears and sharp, watchful eyes. I sniffed up its smell and could tell that it was a male, and not afraid, and hungry.

I growled just a little, letting him know that the paper was mine.

He watched me for a while and decided not to argue. He slinked away, toward the plastic bags, dragging a strange tail, naked of fur, behind him.

That was my first rat. I would meet many others.

I watched the rat move off and decided that this

was the place for me. Here I would be able to do my first, most important job—keeping my stomach quiet.

I would stay here. It would be my new home.

I was not the only animal who wanted to make the place of plastic bags a home.

There were the birds, as I'd seen before, mostly big gray and white ones, always soaring and swooping above the bags, diving in to grab a scrap of this or that. I ignored them. They did not come near me, and there was enough food for us all.

There were rats, of course, and they were more interesting to me. At first I tried to chase them. It just felt like they needed to be chased. But rats were very difficult to catch. They could easily dive into holes in the ground or crevices between bags where I could not follow. So I gave up on chasing and let them be, only growling to warn them if they came too near me while I was eating.

Sometimes, in the night, odd creatures with striped tails came waddling along to investigate the piles. I stayed away from them. They were not as big as I had grown up to be, but they did have sharp teeth. Since I hunted among the piles during the day and they came in the night, we did not have to argue over who was in charge or who got to keep which scrap of food.

But I never saw another dog. I would have liked that. If another dog came here, maybe we could play, as Splotch and I used to. We could do Chase around the plastic bags or find a stick and do Tug-on-a-Stick. We could curl up close at night and keep each other warm.

I missed Splotch. I missed my mother and my brothers. It didn't seem right for a dog to be all alone, with only a growling stomach for company.

Once I glimpsed a new animal among the bags— one bigger than the rats but smaller than me, with striped fur and triangular ears that stuck straight up on her head. A cat! She'd managed to rip open one of the bags and drag out a bone with meat still clinging to it.

I was intrigued. Something told me that this was a different kind of animal from the rats or the nighttime visitors with striped tails. Maybe she was something that might be company.

I went closer. She looked up and gripped the bone tightly in her small white teeth. She put her ears back flat against her head so that her face looked sleek and smooth, and her tail, straight up in the air, fluffed out so that it looked twice as big.

She let out a hiss.

I stopped. That noise was not a growl, but it was pretty clearly a warning. I put my head down low to show her that I was not going to try to take her bone away.

Even though I would have liked it.

But the cat didn't understand what I was so clearly telling her. She backed up a few steps, keeping her wide eyes fixed on me, and then she leaped away and ran.

She wanted to play Chase-Me!

I was happy to oblige. It had been so long since I'd played with anybody! But even though she wanted to play, the cat obviously did not understand the rules, because she headed straight toward the trees that grew beside the plastic bags and raced right up one, snagging the trunk with her claws. In a few seconds she was perched on a branch above my head with the bone still firmly in her mouth.

Unfair! I could not go up the tree after her, so how was this game supposed to work? I put my front paws on the tree and barked a few times, but she didn't come down, so I lost interest and went back to the bags, looking for a bone of my own.

I did not see the cat again. I guessed she was not good company after all.

I'd lived at the place of plastic bags for quite a long time before I first saw the man marching around, kicking at things on the ground.

I did not understand it. Why couldn't he leave this place to me and the rats and the birds and the animals with the striped tails? What was he even doing here? Clearly he didn't come for food. He never ate anything out of the bags. Even so, he seemed to act as if the entire place belonged to him.

Whenever he saw me, he ran at me, yelling angrily and waving his arms. Of course. That seemed to be what people did, whenever they saw a dog near a plastic bag. It made no sense to me: Why put the food out for the dogs and then get so mad when the dog ate it?

I stayed out of his way as best I could. It was hard to do, though, because the magnificent smell of all that trash covered up his scent until he was quite close.

I got even more careful when I noticed that, sometimes, he carried a long stick.

It was different from the stick the woman had used to grab my sister—thicker, not as long, shinier. Still, I did not trust it. One day, when I saw him coming near with that stick in his hand, I squirmed between two plastic bags and held still so he would not see me.

"Where did that stinking dog go?" I heard him grumble as he came closer. "Got to get rid of it."

He kicked one of the bags near me, and I leaped out of my hiding place in a panic. I had to get away!

The man seemed panicked, too. He jumped back with a harsh shout of amazement. He did not have to shout at me! I was already running.

There was a sharp crack from behind, louder than anything I'd ever heard, and the dirt close by my face suddenly jumped up at me! It stung my eyes and hurt my muzzle, and I shied away, running in a new direction. Dirt had never done that to me before!

The man shouted some more, but I dodged around a mound of trash and ran into a clearing behind a small stand of trees, where I knew he could not see me.

I crawled underneath a bush and lay there, trembling.

People. It was important to stay away from people and their sticks.

I must always remember that.

Thinking about sticks reminded me of the last time I saw Splotch, when that woman lowered her stick and snared my sister's neck. I missed Splotch very, very much.

So this was my life: Hiding. Trying to keep the rats and the birds away from my meals. Listening to my stomach complain. And always, always, avoiding people.

Until Megan came.

The first time I saw Megan she was walking with the angry man. He did not have his stick this time, so I was not quite as frightened of him, but I still slunk down behind a truck that was not moving, and stayed quiet so they would not see me.

The angry man seemed to be telling Megan something, moving his hands around in quick impatient gestures as he talked. Megan was nodding.

"I understand," I heard her say as they walked past my hiding place. "But I might not be able to catch her right away. It sounds like she's pretty spooked."

I liked her voice, even then. It did not sound angry. She did not shout. And somehow I felt that she was talking about me. But I still knew better than to let her see me.

Of course, I did not know then that her name was Megan. I did not know why she was there, why she was talking to the man who seemed so furious every time he spotted me.

I let the two people go past and then picked up a bit of moldy potato from a bag near my feet. I took it back to the trees where I had hidden the day the man had yelled and the earth had exploded. I'd gotten used to going there to sleep and eat. I felt safe there, and I trusted that no one could see me.

I gulped down the chunk of potato and curled up for a rest, with my tail over my nose. I dozed a little. Then my ears perked up as I heard footsteps.

I lifted my nose to the breeze. I recognized the smell. Human. Female. A little anxious. There was also something about her—a food smell—that made my nose twitch eagerly. I had never smelled a food smell quite that good before.

Then Megan pushed aside a branch and walked into my clearing.

She stopped when she saw me and stood without moving. I jumped to my feet and stood without moving, too. We stared at each other.

I was tense, quivering, ready to run, but I needed to know which direction to go. What would this woman do? I watched her, waiting for her to make the first move. If she lunged at me, I'd dodge around her and run as fast as I could.

When would she try to grab me? When would she yell in anger, waving her arms? I knew what to expect from humans.

"Oh, honey," Megan whispered. "There you are, right where he said you'd be. Don't worry, now. I'm here to help."

It was odd, hearing a person speak so gently. I'd never heard that before. The woman who brought food to my mother in a metal bowl did not speak to us at all, and most of the other people I'd met shouted.

Megan didn't rush at me, either. She didn't wave her arms or try to scare me.

Instead, she sat down right on the ground. I twitched with surprise.

43

She sat very still.

I watched her for a while.

She kept sitting.

Very cautiously, I lowered my rump to the ground, too. But I was still ready to spring up and dash away as soon as Megan moved.

"There now," Megan said softly. "You're not scared, are you? Such a brave girl. Such a pretty thing, too. Or you will be when we clean you up a little. Are you hungry? I bet you're hungry. That's why you're here. I have something you'll like."

Moving slowly, she reached into a pocket of her jacket. I watched with wide eyes as she drew something out.

A smell drifted off the small square things she was holding in her hand. It was the smell I'd noticed as she approached my clearing.

It made my mouth water. In her hand was something better than moldy potato or greasy chicken or all the other food I'd found in the plastic bags. Something that I wanted.

To my surprise, my tail wagged back and forth.

"Ahh, I thought so," Megan said, still using that soft voice. "You'll like this. Come and try it. Come on, sweetie. I won't hurt you. I'm here to help."

Very, very slowly, she reached out her hand.

Those things in her hand smelled so inviting! I

wanted to go closer. My feet took a step without my telling them to. I could feel my stomach approving of this whole situation.

Megan smiled. "Good girl," she whispered.

I stopped again. Megan was a person, after all. And people shouted and grabbed and had sticks that were frightening.

But Megan wasn't shouting. Megan wasn't grabbing me. And she didn't have a stick.

Instead, she had the little thing that smelled so wonderful. The potato I'd eaten before hadn't satisfied my hunger. My stomach wanted my feet to go and get that thing in Megan's hand.

"That's right. Treat. You want a treat, don't you, girl?" Megan coaxed.

I wondered about that word, "treat." It seemed like it might be important.

Very cautiously, I took a few more steps.

Megan sat still. Her hand didn't waver. I stepped even closer and cautiously nibbled at the tiny thing in her hand.

Treat. This tiny thing must be treat.

Once I had the treat in my mouth, I jumped back. It tasted even better than it smelled! In a moment it was gone, down my throat.

I wanted more.

And Megan had more! She put her hand in her

pocket. In a moment she was holding it back out, *full* of treats.

My tail wagged harder.

"I don't think you're aggressive at all," Megan told me. "I think you're a sweetheart. A hungry sweetheart. That's right, come closer. You can trust me. You know you can. Come on, now, come get the treats."

"Treats." I was beginning to like that word.

I came closer again and took the treats from Megan's palm, retreating back a few more feet to eat them. Megan smiled and held out more. More? This was so exciting. How many treats did she have in that pocket?

I came closer again. It was beginning to feel silly to back away from her each time. Wouldn't it make more sense to stay close to Megan and her treats? This time I ate the treats out of her hand without moving away.

"Oh, good girl. Good girl," Megan murmured.

With the hand that was not holding the treats, she very gently scratched behind my ears.

I froze, startled. No human had ever touched me like that!

"Easy, girl. It's fine," Megan said. "Easy, now."

Her fingers rubbed my skin through my fur.

It felt . . . good. It felt nearly as good as the treats in my stomach. Without even thinking about it, I leaned my head into her hand so that she scratched harder.

Megan laughed, just a little. "Oh, I was right; you are a sweetheart. I bet you want more treats. There you go. Okay. If you come with me, I'll get you some real food, huh? Bet you'd like that. I'm going to get up now, but don't be scared? See, I've got more treats right here."

She pulled some more treats out of that pocket. Wouldn't it work better if she just let me stick my head into the pocket and eat all the treats in a gulp?

Then Megan rose slowly to her feet. I jumped back. Was she going to start yelling now? Did she have a stick hidden somewhere?

But she didn't pull out a stick or make any sudden movements. She just held out that hand with the treats and stood still.

The treats smelled *so good*.

I came closer again. She didn't move. I ate the treats. She didn't move.

I decided that Megan standing up was not really scarier than Megan sitting down. When she started to walk away, still holding more treats in her hand, I followed her.

4

I trailed Megan through the trees and past the piles of plastic bags with all that they contained. A truck was parked along the road. Megan walked to the truck and opened one of the doors.

I hung back and watched warily. Things with wheels were dangerous for dogs.

But this wheeled thing wasn't moving, which probably made it safe. And Megan was standing near it. With treats.

I inched closer.

"Good girl. Brave girl. Now, can you do this?" Megan was saying, still in that gentle voice. "Can you jump right into the truck? Sure you can. Look what I've got for you."

She showed me her hand, full of treats. Then she put the treats inside the truck, on a seat covered in soft fabric.

She stepped back.

"Come on, girl. You can do it. Let's go. This is no place for you, honey. Jump on up. The treats are waiting for you."

I hesitated. I looked at the truck and at Megan.

Then I looked at the road and at the piles and piles of plastic bags. Birds were soaring and swooping over them. Rats were probably crawling among them. In the nighttime the animals with stripy tails would be coming to get their share. Maybe the cat would come back.

But nothing in all of those bags tasted as good as the treats Megan had been feeding me. And nothing sounded as nice as the sound of her voice or felt as good as her fingers scratching behind my ears.

Still, she was a person. She might yell and rush at me. She might find a stick.

And she was standing near a truck. Trucks had wheels.

But this truck had treats, too.

I did not know what to do.

"Don't be scared," Megan whispered. She knelt down on the ground and held out a hand to me. "Come here. You can do it. I know you can."

Step by cautious step, I came closer to her. Her hand had no treats in it now. But it still smelled like them. When I licked her skin, I could taste the treats, along with salty sweat.

She scratched my neck this time. It felt good. It felt very, very good.

"Okay, girl. Good girl. Go on in," Megan told me. "Get your treat."

There was that word again. "Treat."

The treats were in the truck. And now that I was closer, I realized that the inside of the truck smelled like Megan.

Maybe that made it okay. This was not like other trucks.

Just as Megan was not like other people.

I hesitated, and then I jumped. Right up onto the soft seat where the treats had been scattered.

Megan moved smoothly, but not quickly enough to scare me. She closed the door of the truck while I was still crunching up the treats.

I was startled by the bang of the door closing and felt nervous for a moment. I was shut in. There was nowhere to run.

But then Megan opened the other door of the truck and slid in behind a wheel. She closed the door and sighed. I could feel and smell her relief.

"Well, that went easier than I thought it would," she

told me. She pulled a small metal object out of a pocket. I could see it was not a treat, so I wondered why she bothered with it. She stuck it into a hole near the wheel and turned it. The truck made a loud growling sound.

I flinched back against the seat and whimpered.

"Oh, sweetie, don't let the truck scare you," Megan told me. She handed me more treats, which made me feel better at once. "We're going somewhere nice. I promise."

Then the truck started to move jerkily forward. It was hard to keep my balance, so I lay down on the seat and whined again. My ears went flat against my head.

I liked Megan. I liked treats. But I did not like trucks. And I did not know where this one was going.

When Megan stopped the truck and opened the door on my side so that I could get out, the first thing I noticed was the noise. I heard barking, howling, and even some angry growls.

Other dogs!

Megan took me inside a big building and into a pen. The walls of the pen were made of thin strips of twisted wire, just like the fence that used to be around the yard where I'd lived with my mother and litter-mates.

There was something else here that reminded me of the yard—two metal bowls on the floor. One was full of water. And the other had brown chunks in it.

Food!

I trotted over and stuck my muzzle into the bowl. In a few minutes it was empty. When I took my face out of the bowl, Megan laughed. She took the bowl away and brought it back full again, and I gulped the food down just as fast the second time.

It was amazing to feel that my belly was full. Completely full. I could hardly remember the last time that had happened. No longer did my stomach seem like some sort of snarling animal living inside me, constantly demanding to be fed. Now it just felt heavy and satisfied.

Then Megan sat down on the floor and patted a piece of carpet next to her. She talked to me and showed me more treats in her hand. I wasn't as hungry anymore, but those treats still did look and smell good, so I came over and ate some more. Then I sat down on the carpet while Megan scratched my ears and stroked the fur on my back. I wiggled from surprise and pleasure.

I liked being petted. It was new, but nice.

But then something happened that I did not like. Megan scratched behind my ears one last time, and said, "Bye, sweetie, I'd better fill out paperwork for you."

Then she opened up the door of my pen and walked out.

She closed the door behind her.

I was so surprised that I simply sat and stared. I'd gotten into the truck because Megan and her treats were there. I'd gone into this pen because Megan and a bowl of food were here.

But now Megan was gone. Gone!

This did not seem good.

I paced around my pen, trying to learn more about it. The floor under my pads, on the one hand, was cool and hard and smooth. The bit of carpet, on the other hand, was springy but rough. When I smelled the scent rising from it, faint but unmistakable, I lowered my nose, sniffing frantically.

It was Splotch.

Splotch had been here. So had other dogs, and I could tell she hadn't napped on the carpet in a long time, but it was definitely her, my sister. She had come, and now she was gone.

Somehow, that made me feel better about Splotch. We had both been terrified when she had been taken, but if she came here, to this place with treats and Megan, then it hadn't been so bad. This was a place where stomachs could be filled. There was also a bowl filled with water. I lapped some up. It tasted fresh and good.

Oh, Splotch. I missed her so much, but sniffing up her smell on the carpet, I got the feeling that she was happy now. Was she back home with Mother? Was that where Megan would take me next?

I looked around to see if I could get some sense of what might happen to me, and I noticed the other pens. I could see one on either side of me. There were more behind that. Many more.

One of the pens next to me was empty. In the other one was a black dog, a little bigger than me, with short fur and white around his muzzle. He was lying on his carpet, and he picked up his head to look at me but then put it down again. He didn't seem very interested in getting to know me.

This dog was quiet, but other dogs weren't. There were lots of dogs all around. One would bark, then another would answer, and suddenly there would be a burst of barking that didn't die out for a long time.

Some of the barks were angry and even had snarls mixed in. "Don't come near me," those barks said. "Keep away! I'm strong! I'm tough!"

But most of the barks were not like that. Most of them were . . . lonely.

"I'm alone!" those barks said. "Notice me! Stay with me!"

I sat on my carpet and listened to the barking and tried to decide if I liked this new place or not.

It was small, which made me nervous. At the place with the plastic bags or when I'd been roaming the streets with Splotch, I'd had room to run. There had been places to hide if I needed them.

Here I could not run. Or hide.

But there were metal bowls on the floor and Megan had filled them with food. I remembered metal bowls like that from when I had lived with my mother and littermates. People put food in metal bowls.

But not always enough.

Still, Megan was here, and that was a good thing. Well, she was not here right now. She'd left me in this pen, and she'd gone away.

She might come back. But I could not be sure that would happen.

What if Megan never returned? What if the bowls for food stayed empty? I lay on my piece of carpet and nibbled at it, but it did not taste good at all.

After a while, I heard a sound. Slowly I realized that I had heard it before.

It was a pattering sound, like a lot of tiny pebbles were falling down and hitting something hard. It was the sound rain made when it fell and hit the leaves of a tree or a bush that I was trying to hide under.

Rain meant I would be wet and cold. I sighed and wished my sister were still here. Or that I could get out of this pen and huddle with the black dog next door. Even if he wasn't very friendly, he might be warm.

I waited for the rain to hit my fur and soak through to my skin. I waited for the coldness to grow.

But it did not happen.

I was so surprised when I realized that I wasn't getting wet, I sat upright in astonishment. I tipped my head back to see what had happened to the rain.

That's when I figured out that there was no sky overhead. Instead, I saw something big and flat high up in the air.

I didn't know it was called a roof, back then. I just knew it was keeping the rain away.

I lay back down on my carpet, listening to the lonely, frightened dogs bark all around me. But I was not frightened anymore.

This was a good place, I decided. It had bowls for food. It kept the rain from making me cold. And Megan was here, somewhere.

I simply had to trust that she'd come back.

5

Megan *did* come back! And she brought more food! I was so excited that I leaped up from my carpet and danced with happiness. My tail wagged hard enough to make my entire spine wiggle.

Megan laughed. She was happy to see me, too! I gobbled up the food, and then I let Megan pet me. Petting was marvelous. Megan even brought something to help her pet me, something she called a brush. She pulled it through my fur and it felt wonderful, scratching away itches I did not even know I had.

And that was not the only time Megan came back. I saw her nearly every day. She would bring food—wonderful, wonderful food!—and pet me and she'd take me outside.

We'd walk past pens where other dogs lived. I saw and smelled big ones, small ones, shaggy ones whose fur covered their eyes, sleek ones like me, tiny fluffy ones, and one long skinny one with very short legs who yapped to tell me he was the boss every time I walked past his pen.

He was not my boss. I ignored him.

Other cages held animals whose scent I recognized— cats. I used to see and smell cats when I was living in the world with Splotch, and of course I remembered the one who had come to the place of plastic bags. There were tiny cats in some of the cages who looked at me with wide eyes and pretended they were ferocious by showing me their little teeth. They reminded me of the puppy I used to be, and I realized that they were young. Kittens.

Megan would walk with me to a yard where I could see the sky. And if that sky rained at me, I had somewhere to go where it couldn't make me wet! That idea made me so happy, I barked at the sky to show it who was boss. Me!

Then I'd run and sniff hard at the bits of grass and packed-down dirt. Many other dogs used this yard, too, which meant I was busy smelling all the marks they'd left behind.

Megan watched me and laughed. "Oh, Shelby," she said.

Megan said that word a lot. "Shelby, come here," she'd say, and show me treats in her hand. I'd run to her. "Here's your food, Shelby," she'd tell me when she opened up the door to my pen. "Want a walk, Shelby?" she'd ask, and then she'd take me outside to the yard.

I got to like that word. It seemed to mean that something nice was about to happen.

Sometimes a man came along and talked to Megan. He said "Shelby" a lot, too. "Shelby's looking so much better now that you've gotten her cleaned up," he'd say to Megan. Or, "I bet Shelby won't be here long. She's a sweetheart. We'll put a picture of her up on the web-site, and she'll get adopted in no time. You know, we've never—"

"Put down an adoptable animal! Not once since you took charge of the county shelter!" Megan answered him, laughing. "I know, TJ! You know I know!"

They were standing together in the yard while they talked. There were some other dogs in the yard that day, too. Sometimes that happened. We'd sniff each other, and if everybody smelled friendly, there would be the same kind of games I'd had with my littermates—Chase-Me and It's-My-Stick and Wrestle-With-Me-But-Don't-Bite.

Today I was surprised to see that two of the dogs had wheels where their back legs should be! Dogs with wheels? I'd thought wheels were dangerous for dogs. I

60

sniffed these new dogs all over so that I could understand.

They smelled like ordinary dogs—one male, one
female, both older than I was—but they also smelled
of metal and rubber. I realized that their back legs
were actually sitting in little carts while their front
legs touched the ground. It made me think of the
truck ride I'd taken with Megan. It was like these
dogs could take their own truck rides whenever they
wanted to!

They could go pretty fast, too. We played Chase-Me a
bit. But the dogs with wheels would take breaks from
the game now and then to go over to TJ. They'd nuzzle
his hands and look longingly up into his face until he
crouched down to pet them.

I watched with interest. Then I tried it myself. I
trotted over to Megan and looked up into her face.

Megan laughed and bent over to rub my ears with
her fingers. Hah! It worked!

"I can't believe how affectionate Shelby is, after
she'd been a stray. Pretty healthy, too, considering,"
Megan said to TJ. "All she really needed was feeding up."

"How long do you think she'd been scavenging at
that landfill?" TJ asked.

"Months? A year? Hard to know."

Megan took me back to my pen. I noticed that the

dogs with wheels did not go to a pen. They stayed with TJ.

I wondered why.

People who were not Megan or TJ came to my new home sometimes. I would lean up against the door of my pen to watch them.

The people would walk along the rows of pens until they came to a particular one, and then they'd open that pen. The dog inside would come out to greet them.

Some of the dogs came shyly, slowly. Some barreled out with tails wagging. There was always a lot of talking and laughing and barking, and I could tell that the dogs were getting happier by the minute.

Once a dog had greeted people like that, it no longer barked in that sad and lonely way. That dog was happy. I could see it and hear it and smell it. The dog would leave with the people, and I could see happiness in the dog's wagging tail and the head held high.

Even the quiet black dog who lived next to me got to greet someone that way. One day, a man and a woman came to the door of his pen. Their hair was white, just as the dog's muzzle was white. They seemed quiet, too. But when the black dog got up and shook himself and came sedately out of his pen to sniff their hands, his tail began to wag slowly.

They petted him and stroked him. They started to smile.

His tail wagged faster.

They all walked away down the row of pens. No-body walked fast. But everyone was happy.

Greeting dogs made people happy. Greeting people made dogs happy.

I could understand that, a little. I was always happy when Megan brought me my food in the bowls.

But these new people did not bring any food with them at all—not that I could see. And the dogs seemed even happier to greet them than I was to greet Megan!

It was a puzzle, especially since the dogs always left and never came back. Why would they want to leave this wonderful place, where there was food and water and a place to stay dry and warm during the rain? Why would they want to be with any people but Megan?

I began to figure out the answer the day Megan came to my pen and took me out to the yard. TJ was there, but the dogs with wheels were not. In fact, I was the only dog getting outside time.

Some other people were talking with TJ. Two women. One man.

When they saw me, the man started talking very loudly.

"Wow. *Wow*. Amazing. Can you believe it, Cathryn? Look at her! What's her name? Shelby?"

My ears perked up. When I heard "Shelby," some-thing nice usually happened next. Treat?

But nothing particular happened this time. Maybe this man didn't know the rules. He just kept talking. "You were right. She looks exactly like the dog on the cover of the book. I mean, it could be a picture of her!"

The woman standing close to him, who had light-colored hair and kind eyes, laughed a little, too. "You're right. What breed was the dog in the cover photo of *A Dog's Way Home,* Bruce? Did you ever find out?"

"Part pit, part rottweiler, part nobody knows," the man said. I figured out that his name was Bruce. "What's Shelby's breed? Do you guys know?"

TJ shrugged. "Can't say for sure. Pit, we think. Megan says German shepherd, too. Wouldn't be surprised if there's some rottweiler in there, though."

The man named Bruce crouched down and held out his hand to me. "Hey, girl. Hey, Shelby. Come here."

I hesitated and looked up at Megan to check out whether this was okay. I was starting to believe that people were not as frightening as I'd once thought. And Bruce didn't have a stick. Still, he was new to me.

"It's okay, girl," Megan told me. "Here, come with me."

She walked me over to Bruce, and I sniffed his hand.

He smelled interesting, like other dogs and coffee and cream cheese. Megan sometimes smelled like cream cheese in the morning. It was a smell that I liked very much. I licked Bruce's fingers.

The two women came over to meet me and pet me as well. The one called Cathryn said, "Shelby," too, and she stroked my head. The second woman—her name was Teresa—watched closely. Then she put out her hand for me to sniff.

She smelled of other dogs and of dust and wind and sweat and time spent outdoors. I sniffed harder. There was a flowery lotion on her skin, too, and a whiff of something with sugar and cinnamon.

Next I checked out Teresa's boots. They smelled strongly of other dogs, too, just not any I'd personally met. She was very, very interesting.

"Can she do it? What do you think?" Bruce asked Teresa as I sniffed the cuffs of her pants. He reached out to stroke my back while Teresa gently scratched behind my ears. "She looks perfect, but she's never had any training, right?"

I had learned, since meeting Megan, that petting was excellent. But three new people petting me and talking over my head felt like a little too much, even if they did smell of cream cheese and cinnamon and other dogs. I retreated to Megan, who bent down to hug me and talk to me softly. I didn't understand her words, but I leaned into her, content. I knew that her voice was telling me everything would be all right.

I believed her. But I wasn't sure exactly what was happening. Had these three people—Bruce, Cathryn,

and Teresa—come for me? Just as I'd seen people come for other dogs? I was happy to see them, but was I supposed to be very happy? Was I supposed to be wagging my tail and dancing with excitement?

I looked up at Megan, wishing she could tell me.

Teresa was studying me very carefully. I felt as if she wanted me to do something, but I didn't know what.

"What do you think? Can she do it?" Bruce asked again.

Teresa put her hands in the pockets of her jacket. She nodded.

"Look at her," she said, nodding at me and Megan. "There's your answer right there. If Shelby can trust, if Shelby can love, then she can be trained."

She put out her hand. "Shelby, come," she said.

I knew that word—"Shelby." It often had a treat connected with it. But I did not see a treat in Teresa's hand.

I looked up at Megan for guidance. She smiled down at me.

"It's okay, girl. Go on," she told me. She nodded at Teresa.

I didn't always understand the words that people used. But I could tell that Megan wanted me to know something about Teresa.

I thought I understood what it was. She was telling

me that Teresa was a nice person. Like Megan herself. That Teresa was someone I could trust.

Some people *are* nice. Once I had not believed this, but I had learned. Not all people yell and wave sticks and try to hurt dogs. Some of them like dogs. Some even have treats in their pockets.

Bruce and Cathryn and especially Teresa were like that, I decided. They didn't have sticks and they didn't yell. They didn't seem to have treats, either, but maybe that would change. People had ways I did not understand to fill up their pockets with treats. It was probably the best part of being a human person.

Teresa still had her hand out. She was waiting patiently. I walked over to her and sniffed at the hand. Then I sat down at her feet.

Everybody seemed very happy about this. Megan clapped her hands. "That's a girl!" Bruce exclaimed.

Teresa smiled down at me. "This is going to work," she said. "So, Shelby, are you ready to be a movie star?"

6

After that there was some talking. People really do like to talk, much more than dogs do. I've noticed that. Dogs only bark when they have something important to say, like, "Leave my stick alone!" or, "There's a new person at the door!"

But people are different. Sometimes they say important things—like, "Treat!" or, "Walk!" or, "Shelby!," but a lot of the time they just make noises that don't mean anything at all.

Dogs just have to be patient with them.

Finally, Megan took me out of the yard and showed me a small pen that was in the back of a car. What an odd place for a pen! There was a soft blanket on the floor of the pen and Megan offered me a big treat shaped like a bone if I went in, so I did. She shut the door and I looked up at her sadly. I did not really mind being in a pen—big or small—but it was more fun to be where the people were than in here by myself, even with a treat.

"Oh, sweetie, I'll miss you," Megan said. She reached in through the bars of the pen and scratched my ears.

She sounded sad. When I was done with my treat, I'd have to get out of this pen and comfort her.

Then Megan shut the heavy door of the car. That surprised me. It surprised me even more when Teresa slid into the car, too, way up in a seat in front. Bruce and Cathryn and Megan looked in at me through the windows and waved their hands in the air, which made no sense at all.

The car made a growling noise and started moving.

Was this like the truck ride I had taken with Megan on the day I'd first met her? That truck had taken me to my new home, with the pens and all the other dogs and the roof to keep the rain away.

Where would this car take me?

A t first the car did not seem to want to take me anywhere. We drove and drove and drove! Teresa stopped every now and then to take me out and let me pee in the grass by the roadside. She'd talk to me and scratch my ears and say, "Shelby," a lot.

Then she'd put me back in the small pen and we'd drive some more.

But at last the car stopped, and Teresa took me out, and not just to pee. She left the car near lots of other cars and I followed her to a small room. There was carpet on the floor, and in its fibers I could smell that a lot of other people had been here before us. Some of them had dogs with them. I looked around with interest. New friends? But nobody was here now except Teresa and me.

There was a bed in the middle of the room. I ran to jump on it, and it bounced and wobbled under my feet. I looked over at Teresa and let out a single happy bark, trying to tell her I was glad to be here. I was glad to be out of the car. This place had a roof to keep off the rain and I'd be happy to stay here with her.

"Glad you like the hotel, Shelby," Teresa said, smiling.

I liked the room even better when Teresa put down bowls of food and water for me. Bowls! I loved bowls. It was amazing how people could always find bowls and fill them up with food. It was one of the things I liked best about them.

Teresa and I spent that night on the bed. Teresa slept under the blankets and I slept on top of them. It was very nice. I hadn't gotten to sleep next to someone since the day my sister was taken away.

Everything seemed fine. I could not understand it when, in the morning, Teresa took me back out to the car and put me in the small pen *again*.

What was going on? Wouldn't it have been nicer to stay in the room with the bed? The car growled and started moving and I paced as well as I could in my pen. I sat. I stood up. I lay down. Nothing felt right.

Why on earth were we doing this? Why didn't we just stay where we'd been? Or go back to the place with the pens and all the other dogs? Maybe the dogs with wheels would be there. If Teresa saw them, she might understand that dogs didn't need cars to have rides.

I stood up and lay down again. I sighed. I even whimpered a few times.

"Oh, Shelby, not much longer now!" Teresa called back to me. "Don't worry, sweetie; just two more days!"

I didn't know what Teresa was trying to tell me, and I did not like the idea that this car might be my new home. I sighed again.

As it turned out, we stayed another night in a room with a bed. It was wonderful! But the next morning we left, so home was not that room. We were back in the car.

But soon I would find out that my new home was

very different from the car, and from the rooms with the beds, and from the place with all the dogs. It was amazing how many different homes there were in the world!

At last, after much too long, the car stopped and Teresa got out, stretching. She opened up the back of the car and let me out, too.

I peed. Then I sat down gloomily and waited for Teresa to put me back in the pen.

But she didn't. Instead, she clapped her hands to get my attention and led me to a gate in a tall, wooden fence.

"Some new friends back here for you to meet," she said, and opened it up.

Whatever "new friends" were, I could already hear and smell them. They were barking excitedly and jumping up against the gate. Once Teresa opened the gate, I could see them.

"Bode! Luke!" Teresa called out. Two big dogs, muscular and strong, with brown faces and black bodies, hurried to jump up on Teresa. "No, *Off*," she said firmly, pushing them back to the ground. "This is Shelby, boys. Say hi."

I stood still, right at Teresa's side, waving my tail gently, but not too much, lowering my head a bit because I could smell that these dogs lived here. I was in their territory. I wanted to show that I knew that.

The dogs whose names were not "new friends" but were Luke and Bode rushed over to touch noses with me and sniff under my tail. Then they raced away to run circles in the grass and ran back to do it all over again. My tail began to wag harder and harder. Bode's tail, which swept in a circle up over his head, did just the same.

I'd met a lot of dogs in my old home, with Megan, and I'd learned that they were not all friendly. Luke and Bode were. They would not snarl or show teeth. They were happy to see me. They wanted to play!

There was a giant pool of sparkling blue water set into the ground with a long wooden table beside it. A third dog who'd been standing in the shallow end barked loudly. He was brown and black like Luke and Bode and me, but his fur was longer and his ears stood up in stiff triangles on his head. All three of us dashed over to say hello. Luke and Bode were as excited as if they were meeting this new dog for the first time, just as I was—though from the scents painted all over them I knew they had spent many, many days wrestling.

The pool dog leaped out and shook his fur so that water sprayed in all directions. I jumped back and danced in the sudden shower.

"Good boy, Hercules!" called Teresa, laughing. She shut the gate to the yard and came over to another door, a glass one that led into a house. "And now for the last member of the family. Here's Angel!"

She opened the door and a tiny dog shot out, barking at the top of her very small lungs.

I had never seen a dog so small! At first I thought she might actually be one of the rats I used to meet in the place of the trucks and plastic bags, the ones with the skinny, naked tails. But that could not be. She smelled like dog—a female dog, like me.

She could not even reach up to sniff under my tail! When I bent down to sniff under hers, I accidently pushed too hard and knocked her nose-first onto the grass.

She jumped back up to bark at me, and I let my ears droop to show her that I had not meant to be disrespectful.

She forgave me and licked my nose. I licked her ear. Then she raced away to show how happy she was to meet a new friend, jumped into the air, and soared right over Luke's back.

What? I had never for a moment supposed a dog could do a trick like that!

I barked with excitement. How wonderful to be out in a yard with these new friends! And things got even more wonderful when darkness started to fall and Teresa called us in.

It was hard for me to believe, but we did not have to go to our pens! At all!

In the biggest room of the house there was a couch, and all of the dogs piled onto it together. Angel jumped up last and snuggled down into a crevice between Luke's back and Hercules's rump. Teresa patted us all and rubbed our ears. "Shelby, you're going to fit in here just fine," she told me when it was my turn. "You're going to be a wonderful dog."

I wriggled down among them as if I had been sleeping with them my whole life. It felt good to be lying in a heap of dogs. We were together. We were a pack. I used to have a family, with a mother and littermates, but a pack was even better, because dogs in a pack get something dogs in a family do not.

Our own bowls. Our very own bowls!

Teresa lined the bowls up on the floor near the couch and filled them with food and we *all* ate! There was enough for all of us!

I gulped down my food until my stomach was wonderfully full, and then I looked around. All the other dogs were still eating, so I stepped back and went to the water bowl and took a drink.

"Good girl, Shelby," Teresa said, and stroked my head. "You've got lovely manners."

Teresa went into another room and shut the door,

and I spent my first night sleeping together with my pack. My stomach was not angry with hunger. There was a roof over my head, so that even if it rained, I would not get wet. I had friends to play with and to curl up next to at night. I could not remember ever being so happy before.

In the morning, I woke up before any of my pack and squirmed out from under Hercules's muzzle, which was planted in the middle of my back. The big dogs all shifted and sighed and went back to sleep when I jumped to the floor. Angel yapped irritably when she fell off Bode's back and landed on the cushions of the couch, but she curled back up against Luke's flank and settled down.

I was restless and wanted to explore, but the door to outside was closed, so I paced from room to room. I found a room that smelled very strongly of Teresa, but its door was firmly shut as well. I stood outside it for a while in case Teresa came out, but she didn't, so I went on.

Next I found a room that smelled delicious, but that kept its odors hidden behind cupboard doors and inside a big white cold box. I later learned that this room was called a kitchen.

Beside the kitchen was a small sunny room with lots of windows. In a corner of this room was a small pen, even smaller than the one I'd been in for my long car ride. And inside the cage was . . . something.

It looked like a lump of feathers, yellow and tan and blue. And it smelled like a bird. I knew about birds. I'd seen them on trees and in the sky and on the ground, where sometimes it was fun to run at them and bark because they'd flap up into the air and make interesting sounds.

But I'd never seen one in a pen before. I stepped closer. And the bird did something extraordinary.

It pulled its head out from under one wing, and I saw that it had an enormous beak—bigger than any bird I'd ever seen. It looked at me grumpily. And then it let out the loudest *squawk* I'd ever heard in my life.

It was almost as though the bird had barked at me! I was so startled that I barked back! Bode and Luke came barreling into the room to see what the excitement was about. They looked around, saw no threat, and raced back out to run in circles around the couch and bark some more, because it was morning and we were all awake and our pack was together.

"All right, all right," I heard Teresa groan. I heard footsteps on the floor, and a door opened.

Teresa! I wanted to run to her and greet her and check to see if she'd stuffed any treats in her pockets. But I didn't. The bird was still staring at me through the bars of its pen.

I put my rump on the floor and stared back.

What else was there to do? I couldn't chase this bird. I couldn't make it fly up into the air. But it didn't seem right to leave it alone, either. It was strange and big and it had barked at me!

It was important to keep an eye on it.

That's what I did until I heard food being dumped into our bowls. Naturally I had to go and eat. But I did not forget the bird. I'd be back later.

Once Teresa had fed us and petted us and talked to us, she let us all outside into the yard. Wonderful! Games! I showed Hercules how my sister and I used to play I'm-Bigger-Than-You and You-Can't-Catch-Me. Then he jumped into the pool, but I didn't feel like following him.

I'd never seen so much water all in one place before, and I wasn't sure I liked it. Water was for drinking, in bowls or puddles. Jumping into it reminded me of how the rain used to come out of the sky and soak me, and how cold I'd be afterward.

It wasn't cold here at Teresa's house; the sun was fierce and warmed my skin up through my fur. Playing in the yard made me pant and gulp down water from the bowls Teresa kept filled outside. But I still didn't want to go in the pool.

As I watched Hercules swim, something tiny and scaly and low to the ground darted close by my feet and slipped into a crack between two stones. I came over to investigate while Hercules climbed out of the pool, shook hard, and jumped back in again.

Why had he bothered to get out, then?

I put my nose to the crack between the stones and sniffed. Something smelled interesting in there. Animal, but not with fur. I could not get to it. The crack was too small.

I pawed at the crack for a bit, but I could not get a foot inside.

Angel raced up to me and ran beneath my belly. A few feet away, she paused and looked back. I knew she wanted me to play Chase-Me, but next to her was *another* one of those little scaly creatures sitting on top of a flat rock.

It flicked a tongue at me, as if it wanted to lick me. I moved toward it.

It leaped off its rock and dashed away among the sparse grass of Teresa's yard.

So of course I chased it.

The scaly thing ran between blades of grass and I ran after it, but it moved so quickly! Even quicker than the rats I used to meet back at the place of plastic bags. And it shifted directions as if the wind were blowing it from side to side, making my feet slip and skid on the ground as I tried to keep up.

It zipped beneath the fence around Teresa's yard

and was gone. I was so close behind it that my nose banged into the boards of the fence. I sat down and barked in frustration.

Bode ran up to me with a ball between his teeth, so of course we had a good game of It's-My-Ball-You-Can't-Have-It. But right in the middle of the game, another scaly creature actually ran *between my paws!*

Even though we were in the middle of a game, I *had* to chase it. Bode dropped the ball to bark at me, but I was too busy to respond. This time I was so close to the creature that I knew I was going to snap it up any moment! I dove forward and tried to close my teeth on it, but all I got was a mouthful of dirt.

The little thing had raced under Teresa's house and vanished! So unfair!

I heard laughing. Teresa had come out of the house and was watching us play.

All the other dogs rushed over to her and she talked to them and stroked heads and rubbed ears and scratched backs. That looked nice. I hurried over to get my share of attention.

"That's a good girl, Shelby. Good girl, Shelby," Teresa told me, and she nudged Luke aside so that I could squeeze in close to her legs. She crouched down so she could look right in my face and put her hands on each side of my neck to rub my fur with her strong fingers. That felt marvelous! I licked her chin.

"You like chasing lizards, huh? Well, there are a lot of them, so you'll be busy. We're going to get along just fine, Shelby," Teresa told me. "You'll learn to be my dog in no time. And then we can really get started."

I began to understand something then, as the other dogs scattered around the yard to keep playing and I stayed with Teresa for more petting and talking. I didn't just have a dog pack now. I had a person, too. I had Teresa.

That was such an exciting thought that I wiggled all over, from paws to head to tail. Teresa laughed, and I pushed my head under her arm so I could snuggle as close to her as possible. I leaned into her until she nearly fell over. She had to sit down on the ground with me to hold me.

I was like all those other dogs at Megan and TJ's house with all the pens. People had come for me, and now I had a home. This was why those dogs had been so delighted. They were going to a place where they would be loved by a person, and there was nothing more wonderful than that, not even chicken!

A person was even better than a dog pack. A person could scratch behind ears and fill up bowls with food.

And a person did even more than that. A person could give a dog somewhere to belong. I was here with Teresa, in the place with the pool and the lizards and the couch for sleeping, and it was *my* place, in a way my pen had never been, or my spot in the clearing, or even the room with the bed.

Those had been places to stay, but not *my* places. I'd moved on from all of them. But this place—this was mine. Because this person was mine.

I pulled my head back out from under Teresa's arm and licked Teresa's face and hands and enjoyed the taste of her skin—salty from sweat, sweet from some honey she'd eaten for breakfast. "Oh, Shelby!" she told me. "What a love you are, Shelby!"

That was the first time I understood why people kept saying that word around me. "Shelby."

It was my name. I had a person and a pack and a name.

That made me so happy that I had to race around the yard and knock Hercules into the pool and chase three lizards before I ran back to Teresa again.

That night as I lay comfortably on top of Bode and Hercules, something occurred to me. I raised my head and Angel did the same, watching me curiously.

I now understood that when dogs went with Megan to the place of kittens and barking they eventually left and were happy, because they wound up in a home just like this, with people and dogs to love them.

Splotch had been in that same place before I even arrived. That meant she was out there somewhere, curled up on a couch just like this, sleeping on another dog's head just like me. She had her own Teresa. She was safe and happy and loved.

Angel crawled forward and touched her nose to mine, worried something was wrong and keeping me awake. I wagged to let her know that everything was very, very right.

7

So many wonderful things happened in those first days with Teresa, it was hard to keep track of them all. Food in (my own) bowl. Lizards to chase. Lots of petting and talking and chances to hear my name in Teresa's voice. Teresa gave me a present—a collar to wear around my neck with a tag that jangled.

It felt a little funny around my neck at first, and I shook my head hard to see if I could get it off. But it stayed. And I noticed that Luke and Bode and Hercules and Angel had collars like this as well. It must be something that our pack did. After a day or two I got used to it and did not notice it so much anymore.

The collar was a little strange, though I came to like

it. But when Teresa showed me something new—something she called a toy—I knew I'd found the best thing in the world.

"Look, Shelby!" she told me on my third or fourth day at her house. She pulled something out of a rustling paper bag and tossed it into the air. "Here's a toy for you. Catch!"

I jumped up and grabbed it. Of course I did! It was soft and furry and looked a little like a squirrel. Although it did not smell anything like one.

When my teeth closed around the toy, it made a noise. It squeaked!

I was so startled I dropped it and took a few paces back, in case it was going to do something else unexpected. But it just lay there on the floor.

Luke was interested in it, too. He ambled over to sniff at it, and I jumped forward.

That toy was not Luke's. That toy was mine!

I snatched it up right in front of his nose and it let out another squeak. This time I was expecting it, though. I didn't drop it.

I danced away from Luke and shook the toy hard. I don't know why. It just seemed like the right thing to do.

It was quiet. Had I killed it? It didn't smell like something that was alive, but it had made that noise. Often things that made noises were alive. I'd noticed that.

I let the toy drop to the ground. It just lay there. Dead?

I picked it up again. *Squeak!*

This was amazing! It was so exciting that I honestly didn't know if it was a good thing or a bad one. A threat? A game? I couldn't tell! I raced around the house with the toy gripped tightly in my teeth. Luke and Bode chased me, but I never dropped the toy so that one of them could have a turn.

My toy! Mine!

After a while Luke and Bode gave up the chase and I jumped up on the couch with my new toy. I curled up with it and chewed and chewed and chewed.

Squeak! Squeak! Squeak!

It wasn't a threat, I decided. It was a game. It was the perfect game. I bit hard and the toy squeaked at me.

"I may regret this," Teresa said, watching me. But she came over and sat on the couch next to me, stroking my back while I chewed.

How marvelous. My person *and* my new toy, both at once.

Squeak! Squeak! Squeak!

A few weeks after I'd met Teresa, we started to do something new. She called it Training.

Training was confusing sometimes.

On our first day, Teresa came out to the backyard, where I was just about to catch a lizard. She whistled sharply. Every dog's head turned to look at her, including mine.

The lizard dashed through a crack in the fence and vanished. Frustrating! But Teresa was here, and that was even more important than lizards.

She was holding some long ropes in her hands. Later on I learned that those ropes were called leashes, but I didn't know that the first day I saw one.

I ran to Teresa, along with Luke and Bode and Hercules and Angel. When the other dogs saw the ropes, they danced with excitement. Hercules tore himself away from Teresa to race in a big circle around the pool and come back to her feet, panting. I was so fired up I yipped aloud, though I truthfully had no idea what was going on. Bode jumped up to put his front paws on Teresa and grinned in her face.

"No, Bode, Off!" Teresa said sternly. She backed up and he dropped to the ground. I could tell from the droop of his ears and his head that he felt ashamed of himself.

Teresa clipped a rope onto my collar. I was startled and remembered the woman who'd grabbed my sister. She'd put a loop over my sister's neck, attached to a stick.

I knew this was not the same thing. Teresa was

holding a rope, not a stick. And Teresa was one of the good people. I trusted Teresa. I loved Teresa.

But something attached to a loop around my neck still made me nervous. I pulled away from Teresa. I lowered my head and shook it, trying to let my collar slip off over my ears.

"No, baby, it's okay," Teresa said gently. "I know you haven't been on a leash before. Look, Luke will show you. It's okay."

Her voice was gentle, but I was still uneasy. My tail was low and didn't stir.

She clipped one of the ropes onto Luke's collar. Luke didn't seem worried at all. He barked happily and leaned into the rope, trying to pull Teresa over to the gate in the fence.

"Just Luke and Shelby this time," Teresa told the other dogs. "Your turn later."

She tugged gently on the rope around my neck. I braced my feet and didn't move.

"Shelby, Shelby," Teresa said gently. "Come, Shelby. This is okay. Come with me."

I liked to hear my name in Teresa's voice. I moved toward her. Maybe she'd say it again.

"Good girl, Shelby," Teresa said. Luke and Teresa and I all moved together. We walked around the yard slowly. I stayed close to Teresa, and the rope did not tug at my neck.

Luke trotted happily at Teresa's side. The rope that connected his collar to her hand danced in the air.

Oh! A new idea came to me, and it was so surprising that I stopped walking.

The rope connected Luke to Teresa. And it did the same thing for me! When one end of the rope was on my collar and the other was in her hand, she could not go away from me.

Teresa turned to look at me. She pulled very gently on the rope, and I went at once to her side. My tail had started to swish back and forth.

"See there? It's fine. What a smart girl you are, Shelby," Teresa said.

I wagged even faster. I liked Teresa very much. I even liked the rope if it kept Teresa and me close together.

That was the first day of Training. I slowly came to understand that Training was a job.

When I'd been living in the world with my sister or when I'd been at the place of plastic bags, my job had been to fill my complaining stomach with food. It had been such a difficult job, and had taken all my time and attention.

Then Megan had found me and taken me to the building where there were many barking dogs in pens. Food had appeared in my bowl, every day. The job of filling my stomach was taken care of.

Later I had become Teresa's dog. That meant I had *new* jobs to do. Playing with my pack. Chasing the lizards. Staring at the bird in the cage who sometimes barked at me. And, of course, chewing my toy that went *squeak!*

These were all very important jobs, and I did them as well as I could.

But Training was something different. It was better. Because Training was a job that Teresa and I did *together*.

After we'd practiced walking on leashes together for a day or two, Teresa came outside to the backyard. She called to the other dogs and put them in the house, but she didn't tell me I had to go inside.

I was special.

I learned that if Teresa said, "Shelby, Come!" I was to go to her side right away and get a treat. If she said, "Shelby, Sit!" I was supposed to put my rump on the ground and get a treat. And if she said, "Shelby, Stay!" I was supposed to sit and *keep on sitting* until she told me to "Come!"

That one was difficult. I thought Teresa understood that she and I should always be together. Wasn't that why she'd gotten the leashes? But when she said, "Stay!" she walked away from me and I wasn't allowed to go with her.

Even though Stay was hard, I managed it.

Most of the time.

Then a day came when Teresa started teaching me a new job. She put something on the picnic table and tapped it to get my attention. "Shelby, Go Mark!" she told me.

I had no idea what those words meant, but I studied the picnic table with interest. Was there something on it? Something for me? Perhaps a toy that squeaked?

I began to walk toward the table when a lizard darted boldly right under my belly. I leaped after it. Chase! Catch! The picnic table could wait!

"Shelby!" Teresa called firmly. "Go Mark!"

Her voice was loud and clear. The lizard raced up a skinny tree trunk, out of my reach, as I turned my head to look at Teresa.

She was looking at me intently. I looked back. Was there something she wanted?

A smell drifted toward me from the table. Yes! A treat was lying on it. Even better than a lizard! I ran toward the table, jumped up to put my front feet on its surface, and snapped up the treat.

"Shelby, good girl. Good girl," Teresa praised.

I loved her voice when she told me I was a good girl. It was almost as marvelous as a treat.

We did that game a lot. Teresa seemed to like it. I thought it was not quite as much fun as being connected to Teresa by a leash . . . but there was a treat involved, so I was happy to play. "Go Mark!" Teresa would tell me, and I would dash over to the picnic table from wherever I was in the yard. There was always a treat waiting for me.

Of course, sometimes there were lizards, too. Lizards did need chasing. Or the other dogs would bark at me from inside the house and I'd run up to the door to bark back, wondering when we would all play together again.

But Teresa did not want to give up the game. "Shelby, Go Mark!" she'd tell me.

There was something in her voice when she said it. She wasn't angry with me or being fierce, but she meant what she said.

It reminded me a little of how my mother would bark or growl, just a tiny bit, if my littermates or I bit one of her ears and pulled too hard or decided to chew on her feet. We learned to stop, right away, when our mother told us to.

When Teresa used that voice, I was supposed to do what she wanted. When I did, she was so pleased with me that it made up for the lizards I didn't get to chase.

I loved making Teresa happy. Even when she changed the game.

After a few days of running to the picnic table, I came outside with Teresa and she told me, "Go Mark!"

I ran to the picnic table. I knew what to do.

But there was no treat! I turned to Teresa, bewildered. What had happened to our game?

"Shelby, Go Mark!" Teresa said again. She was watching me closely.

I looked around, baffled. Then the breeze brought an enticing scent to my nose.

There was the treat! It was sitting on a big square piece of wood on the ground. I ran to it and gobbled up my reward. Teresa patted me and praised me, and then we did it some more.

Honestly, lizards were still more exciting.

After we'd played Go-Mark for a while, Teresa and I did a new game. "Up, Shelby! Up!" she said, coming close to me and patting her chest.

I just stared at her, baffled. She bent down and picked up my front legs, putting them near her shoulders.

"Good girl!" she praised. I got a treat.

When Luke or Bode did that, Teresa told them, "Off!" and pushed them away. But when I did it, I got a treat!

I knew for sure that I was Teresa's most special dog. The next time she told me, "Up!" I leaped up right away so I could lick her face and show her that I loved her as much as she loved me.

Another day, when Teresa and I came outside, there was a big wooden box in the corner of the yard. I ran to it and sniffed it to see if it was interesting, but it wasn't.

Teresa dropped something on the ground—a rubber bone! I grabbed it happily. The other dogs were inside, so we couldn't play It's-My-Toy-You-Can't-Have-It, but maybe Teresa would do it with me.

Teresa stood over by the box and clapped her hands. I perked my ears up at the sound. "Pick It Up! Put It in There!" she called out.

I came over to her side so that I could show her the bone. Didn't she want it? Wouldn't she chase me?

"Put It in There!" Teresa said, pointing. Her hand was actually inside the box, and she was using her Training voice. I knew she wanted me to do something. But I didn't know what.

Then I saw that she had a treat in her hand. One of the best things about Training was that it involved so many treats! I stuck my head into the box to get at the treat. I dropped the bone from my mouth so that I could nab the treat from Teresa's hand.

The bone hit the bottom of the box with a thump, and Teresa opened her hand to let me get at the treat. "Good girl! Good girl, Shelby!" she told me. She scratched behind my ears.

Then she took the bone out of the box and tossed it away across the yard. "Pick It Up! Put It in There!" she told me.

What? Didn't she want the bone to be in the box? She'd told me I was a good girl for dropping it there, but then she'd thrown it away.

How confusing. I ran to get the bone. Then I settled down to give it a good chew.

"Shelby! Put It in There!" Teresa called out.

I looked up at her. She'd said my name. What did she want? I went to her side to see. I dropped the bone on the ground at her feet and nuzzled her hand so she'd remember that dogs need petting.

(People need a lot of reminders about this.)

Her hand smelled like treats. I licked it. Then I sniffed at her pockets. I could smell that she had more treats somewhere. The thought made saliva start to gather in my mouth.

"Nope, no treat yet," Teresa said to me. "Pick It Up! Put It in There!"

I tilted my head. What did she want me to do? Maybe she wanted to play. I took up the bone in my mouth again and showed it to her. Chase?

"Put It in There!" Teresa said, pointing to the box. Her hand was over the box now. Did that hand have a treat in it again?

I went to the box and stretched out my neck so that I could get close to Teresa's hand. I pushed at her hand with my nose.

"Put It in There!" Teresa repeated.

I dropped the bone in the box so that I could lick Teresa's hand.

"Good girl! Good girl, Shelby!" Teresa told me.

Then she remembered to give me a treat. At last!

8

Teresa and I played Training quite a lot. Sometimes other people joined us. Their names were Brian and April. They were kind and I could smell that they spent a lot of time around dogs, some of whom I'd never met. But no one was as special as Teresa.

We played Go-Mark very often, even though Teresa seemed to forget the rules a lot. First Go Mark meant "Run to the picnic table and get a treat!" Then it meant "Run to the piece of wood on the ground and get a treat!" I guess Teresa kept losing the piece of wood, because day after day she'd have to find a new one so that we could play the game. Each new piece would be smaller than the one before.

At last Teresa found a piece of wood that she could keep track of—a small disc about the size of one of my paws. Whenever she'd tell me, "Shelby, Go-Mark!" I'd find that disc and stand on it until she came to tell me what a good girl I was and how smart I was.

Sometimes Teresa even forgot the treat! It's funny how humans can be so clever about some things—like opening cans of dog food or doors to the outside world—and so confused about others. But I always did Go-Mark right, even if Teresa didn't. And she was always pleased with me.

One day, Teresa put the leash on me so that we'd stay together and she took me out to the car. I jumped in happily and sat in the backseat while she sat in the front. Things with wheels didn't worry me any longer, as long as Teresa was nearby.

We drove and drove, until I got tired of sticking my head out of the window to sniff all the rushing smells, and curled up on the soft seat for a nap. When I woke up, the car wasn't moving any longer.

"Okay, Shelby, we're here," Teresa said.

She opened up my door and took my leash. I leaped down and smelled something amazing.

It smelled . . . huge. And salty. And damp. I looked around in confusion. We were in a parking lot with a lot of other cars but no buildings. There was space and light everywhere, and small hills to one side. That gigantic smell came wafting at me over those hills. A sound came from that direction, too—a sort of growl that pulsed louder, softer, louder again.

I began to pull Teresa that way, eager to see what could be making such a salty odor. "Okay, take it easy; that's where we're going!" she said, coming along behind me.

We took a sandy path over the hills and I saw what I'd been smelling and hearing. Water! So much water! It stretched out ahead of me to the horizon and to either side as far as I could see. And it moved in a very funny way. The water in Teresa's pool jumped and rolled when Hercules leaped into it, but this water heaved *itself* up in hills and then flattened itself out again as it slid up a long stretch of wet, sloping sand. I was amazed—did Hercules know about this place?

Birds were swooping and soaring over the water, and people were walking beside it. Some of the people had dogs with them. New and fascinating scents rushed to my nose—salt and seaweed and people and dogs and sandwiches and potato chips from a family that was having a picnic nearby and something sort of like the fish Teresa sometimes ate for dinner and many, many more that I couldn't identify.

It was so exciting that I danced on the end of my leash and Teresa laughed at me. She waved at one of the walking people who was connected to her dog by a leash. "We're here!" she called.

This new person came over to us. I knew her—it was April! And she had another dog with her! He was a shaggy brown male with a white blaze down his face. He was both bigger and older than me. In fact, he was gigantic! Angel could sleep several nights on top of him and never be in the same spot twice!

"Here's Gusto!" April said.

"Let's let them get used to each other a bit," Teresa said, loosening up my leash so that I could get near to this big dog and smell him properly.

He was calmer than I was. I frisked around him, sniffing all the right places, but after a few polite sniffs he sat and looked up at April, as if waiting for her to tell him what to do next.

But I knew what to do next! We should run! There was all this sand. It would be excellent for a game of You-Can't-Catch-Me. And there were birds! We should chase the birds. They were not as good as lizards, but they'd do.

I stretched out my front legs in front of the new dog, Gusto, and bowed down so that he'd get the hint that it was playtime. But he just looked at me. Some dogs are all business. I guessed Gusto was one of them.

That was okay. I still had Teresa. I straightened up

and tugged at the leash and looked up at her. Chase-Me? Now?

Teresa did not get the hint. "There they are," she said. She waved again at two more people and they came over to us, walking a little unsteadily on the sand. I'd met them before, back at the place with all the dogs in pens. Bruce and Cathryn!

"Wow, Shelby looks amazing!" Bruce said. He crouched down to greet me and rub both his hands in the fur around my neck. He was pretty good at it. Not as good as Teresa, of course, but acceptable. "You've gained weight. You look so healthy!" He glanced up. "How's her training coming?"

"She's a smart girl," Teresa said, smiling. I pulled away from Bruce's hands and went over to her. I knew the words "smart girl." They were almost as nice as "good girl." And they often came with a treat.

Not this time, though. Oh well.

"This is new to her, though," Teresa went on, still talking to Bruce and Cathryn. "Gusto's an old pro, but we'll see how Shelby does."

She took a small plastic container out of her pocket and showed it to me. My tail began to *whap* back and forth with enthusiasm. Inside the container were treats! One of the very best things about Teresa was how often she had treats in her pockets.

April gave Gusto's leash to Cathryn to hold, and he

sat calmly watching as April took a small shovel out of a backpack and dug a hole in the sand.

I wanted to go over and sniff at the sand, but Teresa still had the container of treats in her pocket. So I stayed with her.

Life is full of difficult choices like that.

Then Teresa tossed the treats to April. Wait! That was not right! Treats were for dogs, not people!

Teresa seemed to know how I felt. She stroked my head and smiled down at me. "Just a minute, girl. Don't worry."

April pitched the container into the hole and then began to pile the sand back in on top of it. How strange people were. First April dug the hole; then she filled it in!

"Okay, Shelby. Okay, Gusto," said Teresa. "Dig!"

She nodded at Cathryn, and Cathryn let go of Gusto's leash at the moment that Teresa let go of mine. We both knew just what to do. We ran to the spot where April had filled in her hole and started to paw frantically. There were treats down there!

"So what's this for again?" Bruce asked, while Gusto and I sent sprays of sand between our back legs. "There's nothing in the movie script about digging something up on the beach."

"The avalanche scene," Cathryn said. "When Gusto

and Shelby have to dig the victim out of the snow? You remember? You wrote the book, after all."

"But this is sand, not snow," Bruce said. He sounded puzzled.

My claws scraped on something plastic. The container! I'd found it! Gusto pawed right next to me, and in a few seconds we had it uncovered. I grabbed it up in my mouth before he could get it, and pranced around, showing it to him. Now maybe he'd play?

"Good dog, Shelby. Good dog, Gusto," Teresa said. "Okay, Shelby, give me that." She held out her hand for the container. I was disappointed. I could smell the treats and almost taste the treats, but I couldn't get them out. It wasn't worth all the digging after all! I let Teresa take it.

Then Teresa—wonderful Teresa!—opened up the container and shared the treats with Gusto and me. "Well, we don't have snow in Los Angeles, so this is the closest thing," she said to Bruce while she was doing this. Her voice was extra-patient, as it was sometimes with me when we were doing Training and it was hard for me to figure out what she wanted me to do. Bruce, I decided, was very much like a dog finding it difficult to learn new tricks.

"We've got to practice somewhere," she went on. "The two avalanche scenes are going to be Shelby's biggest challenges. She starts out trying to free herself from the snow—though she'll actually be in a big buried box and will just climb up a ramp and out. But then comes the most important stunt she has, where she helps Gusto find the victim in the snow and dig the guy out. If she doesn't get that scene right, we're going to have a real problem."

"Shelby's so smart," Cathryn observed.

Teresa nodded. "She is, but I like to train my dogs so that they've practiced exactly what they're going to be doing in the movie. For this scene, though, pawing through wet sand is as close as we can come." She shook her head. "Shelby loves to please people, so she's very trainable, but she's still young. I hope she can figure it out when we're actually shooting."

They were saying my name a lot. I gave Gusto a smug look—clearly I was the most important dog today!

Teresa shook more treats into the container, and April began to dig another hole. It's very odd how humans like to do the same things over and over again. Teresa tossed the container into the hole, and April piled the sand over it once more.

"Dig!" Teresa told Gusto and me.

We dug. The hole was deeper this time, and it took us longer to get to the treats. Wouldn't it have been easier just to put the treats on top of the sand and skip all that digging? And why would anyone bury a treat when it was so much nicer just to eat it?

It turned out that Dig was a game kind of like Go Mark, where the humans kept forgetting the rules. First Gusto and I did Dig together. Then Teresa kept hold of my leash while Gusto did Dig. I squirmed restlessly by her side. What if Gusto dug up all the treats? What if this was something like what used to happen in the yard with my mother and my littermates, when there wasn't enough food for all?

"Wait, Shelby. Wait," Teresa said softly to me. Her voice was soothing. "You'll get your turn."

Gusto did get treats! Unfair! April took him to one side to eat up his reward, and Teresa let me go.

I leaped into the hole that Gusto had started and dug and dug. "Whoa!" Bruce said, jumping out of the way of the sand I was throwing up. I didn't feel bad for spraying him with wet sand—he had to know we were doing Dig, and if he didn't, perhaps he shouldn't be standing so close to the hole.

There were treats in the hole for me, too! I felt much better after Teresa pulled them out of the container and gave them to me.

Then the people changed the game *again*.

April dug another hole and buried the treats, but this time something very odd happened. When Teresa told Gusto and me to Dig, a loud buzzing sound came out from under the sand!

I was so started I jumped. Bruce did, too.

"What's that?" he asked.

"It's a buzzer," Teresa said. "I don't know if the dogs will be able to smell the treats under the snow later on. But they can certainly hear a buzzer. If they learn to associate the treats with the buzzer, that will help."

I was puzzled by the strange sound, but Gusto started doing Dig with no hesitation, so I did, too. Last time there had been enough treats for everyone, but there was no guarantee that would happen this time, as well. I couldn't let him get ahead of me.

We found our way to the treats again, and there were enough for both. What a relief! In fact, I began to get a little full of treats. Treats taste amazingly fantastic when your stomach is empty. When your stomach is full, they simply taste normal fantastic.

And I hadn't chased the birds yet. They kept swooping low over our group, as if they wanted treats for themselves. When I barked at them, they'd soar away, but they always came back. Birds are not very bright. Perhaps that's why Teresa kept hers in a cage, to keep it from bothering good dogs during Training. I needed to let them know who was in charge, the way I had taught the lizards in the yard to respect me.

So the next time the buzzer went off and Teresa told me, "Dig," I dashed away to teach those birds a lesson.

"Shelby, no!" Teresa shouted. "Shelby, Come!"

But I had to show one very large bird with a hoarse squawk that he was not in charge here. I chased him off and came back to Teresa, expecting praise and treats.

Gusto was done with Dig. He had sand all over his nose and was eating the treats Teresa had given him.

I looked up at Teresa pleadingly. Surely she'd see how I'd taken care of that bird for her. Surely she'd give me a treat.

But she didn't! Oh well. I was getting tired of Dig anyway. It was more fun to learn new tricks than to do the same one over and over.

"I think Shelby's getting bored," Teresa said.

I yawned. If we weren't going to chase birds, all the loose sand would make for a very nice nap.

"Let's change things up for her," Teresa decided.

The people talked a little more, and then Bruce picked up April's shovel and started digging. Were we going to *keep* playing Dig? What about our other games? What about Go Mark? I was very good at that one.

And I was excellent at chasing birds.

Bruce didn't know how to dig right. He worked hard at it, but unlike April, he made a hole that was wide and shallow instead of one that was narrow and deep. Then he lay down in his hole—so *Bruce* got to take a nap? Why should he get a nap? He didn't have any real jobs to do, unlike Gusto and me!

April and Cathryn piled sand on top of Bruce in a high mound. His head and face stuck out at one end, and his feet could be seen at the other. "Okay, Shelby. Dig!" Teresa called.

April kept hold of Gusto's leash. *This job was just for me.*

I went over and sniffed at the mound of sand suspiciously. I supposed digging up a person might be an interesting change from digging for treats, but even when I heard the buzzer I couldn't get myself to do it. I was tired from all the digging, and I had seen Bruce dig a hole and lie in it. If he was dumb enough to do that, having a dog dig him back up wasn't going to help.

"This doesn't seem to be going well," Bruce remarked from where he was lying on the sand.

Cathryn looked to Teresa. "But when we shoot the avalanche scene, it won't be a real person. It will be a dummy, right?"

Teresa nodded. "I just wanted to change things and see how Shelby reacted. Everyone is saying this is the one scene she can't screw up—but it is the one scene I can't practice for. I was hoping she would decide to dig Bruce out of the sand. This really worries me."

Everyone was quiet. I yawned.

"Bruce," Cathryn said, "Shelby doesn't think you're a dummy."

"Smart dog," he replied.

People laughed, but I was watching Teresa, who was frowning at the sand. "Hope we can make it work," she muttered.

Bruce stood up out of the sand, brushing himself off. As far as I was concerned, it proved he didn't need my help.

No one gave me a treat, though.

9

Not long after that day near the water where Gusto and I did all the digging, I got to take a long car ride with Teresa. Just me—not the rest of the pack. They stayed home.

It was because I was Teresa's most special dog, of course. I sat in the backseat and Teresa left the car window open just a little for me. I loved being the special dog! I put my nose up to the crack and joyfully breathed in all the scents from the world outside and felt so happy to be going somewhere—anywhere—with Teresa.

As the car rolled on and on, I noticed that the land around us changed. At first it was hot and dry and mostly flat. Then I began to feel the car going up and down more and more hills, and I noticed a new odor coming in through the window.

It was a smell that was fresh and chilly and damp and new to me. It made my tail wag and my ears perk up. What was this? When would I find out?

When Teresa stopped the car at last, I learned what the new smell was.

She opened my door for me and I scrambled out to find my paws buried in something white. My first thought was that it must be something to eat. I took a bite. It tasted like the water in my bowl—but cold! Freezing! My teeth and tongue ached. I shook my head and most of the white stuff fell out of my mouth.

"Snow, Shelby. It's snow!" Teresa said.

Snow? Was she talking about the white stuff? It was cold on my feet! I lifted each paw, one after the other, and shook it. But that didn't help, because I had to put my paws back down again, right into the white stuff.

"Well, you were born in Tennessee, and you've been living in the desert—I guess snow does come as a shock," Teresa said. "Come this way. I want you to meet somebody, and we thought a park was a good place."

She'd said that word again. I was beginning to understand that the white stuff was called snow. What was it used for? Clearly it wasn't to eat.

I lifted each foot high as I followed Teresa out of the parking lot and into a place with swings and a slide and a structure made of bars. Lots of children dressed in brightly colored, puffy clothes were running and climbing. Some were clambering up small mountains of the white stuff and sliding back down.

Someone waved to Teresa and me—a tall young man with fair skin and dark hair. He knelt down right in the snow and held out his hands to me. Teresa let go of my leash, so I knew I had permission to run to him.

I liked him! He had strong fingers that knew how to scratch my fur and he talked to me in an excited voice. Later on I heard a lot of people calling him Lucas, so I figured that was his name.

"We're going to do lots of scenes together, huh, Shelby?" Lucas told me. "You're the real star of the movie, you know. Hey, Shelby, want to run? Come on, chase me, Shelby!"

He got up and ran a little way away, looking back at me to see if I was following. This was a human who knew how to play Chase-Me properly!

Of course I wanted to play. I'd been sitting in that car for such a long time! Running was hard in the snow, which came up to Lucas's ankles and over my paws. But I learned to jump through it, a little like Hercules swimming in the pool back home. Then Lucas fell down on his back in the snow and I leaped on him to lick his face and check out whether he had any treats in his pockets.

He rolled over. I wiggled after him and rolled over, too. That's when I figured out what the snow was for.

It was for playing in!

Snow was soft and fluffy and even better to dig in than the sand at the beach. Plus, it tasted much better than the sand. I learned not to keep snow in my mouth, but just to snap at it and let it go. I left Lucas's side and raced away from him, just to feel the white stuff crunch under my feet.

Lucas, still sitting in the snow, picked some up and packed it into a ball between his mittened hands. Then he threw it.

I knew what to do with balls! I ran after this one, watching as it arced through the sky. I saw where it would fall to earth and I put on a little extra speed so I would meet it.

It hit the ground and . . .

Where was it? I skidded to a stop, looking around, baffled. I'd *seen* the ball hit the ground. But I couldn't find it now.

Lucas was laughing. Why didn't he help me find the ball instead of sitting there?

Never mind. I could figure this out. The ball must have gotten buried in the snow. I'd dig for it!

I jumped to where I'd last seen the ball and clawed at the snow. It flew around me in showers. But I never did find that ball. How irritating!

"Watch Shelby for a minute!" I heard Teresa call to Lucas. "I want to get something from the car!"

I wrestled with Lucas in the snow until Teresa came back.

"She's already digging," Teresa told Lucas. "So we could get a little extra practice in for that avalanche scene. This is her first time in snow, and she's doing great! Let's take advantage of it. Play with her some more while I bury the buzzer."

Lucas and I roughhoused some more, and I won. I was sitting on him when I heard Teresa call from a few yards away.

"Shelby! Dig!"

I jumped off Lucas, who let out his breath in an *ooof* sound, and ran to Teresa's side. She had used her Training voice. I knew I had to pay attention to it.

But it seemed like a funny command. Dig? There wasn't any sand. What was I supposed to do?

I looked up at her for a clue.

"Shelby, Dig!" Teresa said firmly.

Had she gotten mixed up? Did she think we were at the beach? Anyway, where was Gusto? Didn't we play Dig with Gusto?

I heard a familiar sound. Something went *buzz!*

My ears perked up. I looked around. There would be sand somewhere, and I'd do Dig, and Teresa would tell me I was a good dog.

But . . . where *was* that sand?

Lucas came panting up to us as I hunted for sand. He started to ask something, but Teresa made a quick gesture with one hand, and he got quiet.

Teresa was looking at me seriously. The buzzer sounded again.

I took a step toward where I heard the noise. The buzzer was under the snow.

And I could dig snow, right? I'd just been digging in it to find that ball that Lucas had thrown.

I hadn't found the ball. But I could find the buzzer. I'd find it, and Teresa would be happy, and there would be treats!

I hurried to where I'd heard the sound. My front feet sank into the fluffy snow, and I dug and dug. It was a little different from digging in the sand, because the snow packed down and got harder under my feet as I went deeper.

But I didn't give up. I was a good dog, and I knew how to do Dig, and I'd find that buzzer!

And I did. My claws scraped it up, and Teresa was right there next to me, to praise me and give me a treat from her pocket.

I wagged up at her happily. Then we played Dig lots more, and I always reached the buzzer and got my treat. Lucas seemed just as happy as Teresa every time I dug it up.

"She's going to be great!" he told Teresa.

"I hope so," Teresa said seriously. "But it'll be different at the shoot. Gusto will be there, too . . ."

I heard Gusto's name and looked around, but I didn't see or smell him anywhere nearby.

". . . and there will be new actors that she's never met. We'll just have to see how it goes."

Lucas stroked my head. "It's your big scene, Shelby. I know you can do it!"

I guess Teresa thought the snow was as much fun as I did, because the next day we drove some more, up and up and up the side of a very big hill to a place where there did not seem to be much besides snow and trees.

Oh, and people.

The trees were tall and dark, with long needles and a sharp smell that tingled in my nose. The snow was packed down hard where all the people had been walking but fresh and fluffy where they had not. I loved jumping into big piles of it, just like Hercules jumped into the pool back at Teresa's. But snow was better than the pool because it was easier to climb out.

The people all seemed busy. Very, very busy.

They were dressed in bright, puffy clothing, like the children I'd seen at the park. And they were doing jobs, just as I was when I did Training with Teresa. I could tell that by how serious they were, how focused on what they were doing.

As far as I could figure out, their jobs were mostly to walk back and forth, carrying things.

They carried clipboards. Pieces of paper. Tall ladders and platforms and long metal arms that could be hoisted up into the air. Giant lights on skinny legs. Cups of coffee. Many of the people had big, funny-looking black boxes that they spent a lot of time staring at. They were like phones—I'd seen Teresa look at her phone often—but bigger. I never understood why people spent so much time staring and poking at phones when there were dogs available for petting and playing, but they did.

Other people had different kinds of black boxes with tubes sticking out from them. They called those boxes cameras.

There were tents, too, arranged around the edges of all the activity, and Teresa took me to one of them. There were already people inside it, sitting on stools—Brian and April! I was so excited to find old friends here in this new place that I ran to them. Even without Teresa telling me to do Up I jumped to put my feet in their laps and lick their faces.

Brian and April laughed and hugged me back. Then I hurried away to sniff around the tent. Along one side were some boxes in a corner that smelled like Teresa's house. One had a rip in a corner and inside it I could catch the scent of my squeaky toy.

I pawed at the box to see if anyone would notice and get my favorite toy out for me, but Teresa and Brian and April were talking and nobody did. I left the box reluctantly and investigated the rest of the tent.

There was a very nice lamp low to the ground that beamed down heat as well as light. Sitting in front of it felt like sitting in the sun in Teresa's backyard. In front of the lamp was a thick blanket for me to lie on. That was nice. I liked the snow, but my feet did get cold in it after a while.

"Look what Brian has for you, Shelby," Teresa told me.

I recognized Brian's name, so I glanced at him. He opened up a box and pulled out a big blue something. And then four small black somethings.

"Here, let's try them on," Teresa said, and she knelt down beside me.

The big blue something went over my back. It was soft and smooth and felt very cozy when Teresa pulled the straps tight.

It was a coat, I realized! Just like the ones April and Brian and Teresa were wearing. I had a coat of my own.

Then Teresa took one of the small black things. She picked up my foot and slipped the thing on.

I shook my foot. The black thing did not fall off.

I put my foot down to sniff at it. It smelled odd—sort of like cloth and sort of like plastic. I nibbled it. It did not taste good.

"No, Shelby, leave your boots on," Teresa told me. "They'll keep your feet warm and safe from the ice, too."

I looked at her, wondering what she was talking about and why she was putting these odd things on my feet. It was nice having her face so close to mine, though. I licked her ear.

April helped Teresa put the three more black things on my other paws. I took a few steps in them, lifting my feet high to see if I could step out of them.

I couldn't. I sat down and looked up at Teresa.

"You'll get used to them, sweetie," she told me, and looked over at Brian. "About time for her first scene, right?"

Brian nodded, and Teresa took me back out of the tent, right in the middle of all the hurrying people.

It felt so funny to walk in the boots! I couldn't feel the cold snow under my feet. That was . . . good? Maybe? But I couldn't use my claws, either, if I started to slip. What if I needed to run fast? What if they wanted me to do Dig?

The coat, though—I loved the coat. It was snug and warm and I felt so happy in it that my tail swished

through the air and *whapped* against people's knees as I walked.

Teresa took me to a patch of deep, fresh snow. I wiggled with excitement. Would I get to play in it?

Several people were standing nearby as if they were waiting for us. Some of them had clipboards. Some had the big black boxes I'd noticed earlier. One was standing near a long metal arm with a camera on the end of it.

Teresa bent down and took off my coat and my boots. Maybe she understood how funny the boots felt.

Then Teresa took something out of her pocket. It was the wooden disc that we used to do Go Mark.

I understood right away that we were not playing. We were Training. It seemed funny to be Training in front of all these people. But I could show them all that I knew how to do Go Mark.

Teresa took the disc and put it on top of a big snowbank, making sure that I could see it. Then she came back to my side.

"Okay, this is it, girl," she told me, looking down at me. "Shelby, Go Mark!"

I knew exactly what to do! I leaped into the deep snow and plowed straight through it. All the people stood around and watched me. The camera on the metal pole swung around to follow me as I ran.

When I reached the slope of the snowbank, I scrambled up. Teresa must have known I'd need my claws for this—that was why she'd taken those funny boots off! At the top, I found the Go Mark and stood right on it. I paused and looked back at Teresa.

"And . . . cut!" somebody said.

"Shelby, good girl!" Teresa said warmly. I bounded down off the snowbank straight to her, and she rubbed her hands through my fur and gave me a treat, just like she always did.

10

"That was great! She did it!" exclaimed a familiar voice. I looked up and saw Bruce standing next to Teresa. It was funny how so many of my old friends had come to this mountain. Maybe it was because they wanted to see how good I was at Training.

"Shelby's a natural," Teresa said warmly.

"She's a star!" Bruce knelt down in the snow to say hello, and I gave his chin a lick to be polite. "What's up with that little wooden thing?" he asked Teresa. "Why can't she just go to you or April?"

"She's been learning to Go Mark pretty much since the first day I started training her," Teresa told him. I looked around alertly. Was I supposed to go back to the disc? But Bruce kept scratching my neck and ears, so I guessed not right at that moment. I didn't get petted when Training was happening.

"It's about the most important thing a movie dog needs to know," Teresa went on. "She can't just run to me or April or Brian because we can't be in the shot. And often the script calls for her to get somewhere and do something—pause or turn or dig something up, or whatever. So she can't just keep running out of the frame. She's got to get to where the camera needs her to be, and then she's got to stop. That's how we get the shots we need."

"Okay, the next shot is over by the trees!" someone called out.

"Come on, Shelby, time to work," Teresa said.

Bruce wanted to keep petting me, but I was busy. I had Training to do with Teresa. Bruce was nice, but he didn't always understand that I had a job to do.

We did a *lot* of Training that day. Over and over I showed all the people who wanted to watch me that I could do Go-Mark, no matter where Teresa put the little piece of wood. I did Go-Mark under trees and on big fields of snow. I raced up a hill and found my Go Mark on top of a big rock. Once I got there, I stood on top of the rock and barked as long and as loud as I could.

Cathryn and Bruce had come to watch. "This is for the scene with Big Kitten," I heard Cathryn tell Bruce. "You know, when the coyotes back the dog up against the rock and then Big Kitten comes and scares them away."

I knew what a kitten was. There had been some in the place with all the dogs in pens. But I didn't see or smell any kittens, so I didn't know what the humans were talking about.

It didn't matter too much, because I got a treat from Teresa and praise for finding my Go Mark from April and Brian. Bruce told me over and over what a good dog I was. He found a stick and we wrestled with it. I guessed that's why he'd come to this mountain, to play with me, because he didn't seem to have much else to do with his life.

If he needed a job, I wished he'd go and get my squeaky toy out of the box in our tent. But he didn't seem bright enough to figure out where it was. I felt a little sorry for him, even though Cathryn seemed to be his person and she was very nice. I wondered if Cathryn had found Bruce the way Megan found me: living in a place with plastic bags and birds and rats.

After I won Tug-on-a-Stick with Bruce, Teresa took me to one side of a big field of snow. I saw April on the other side. She waved and called my name. I looked up at Teresa.

Teresa nodded down at me. "Go, Shelby!" she said. She snapped off my leash. "Go!"

That was great! I loved leaping through the snow, kicking up big sprays from under my claws. The snowflakes showered all over my fur and quickly melted, soaking me down to the skin. I bounded to April's side and someone yelled, "Cut!"

April told me I was a good dog and gave me a treat from her mittened hand. "Better dry you off," she told me. She had a nice warm towel over her arm, and she put it over me and rubbed and rubbed.

I wiggled with happiness and licked her face to show them how much I appreciated all the attention. Maybe that's what "Cut!" meant—"Rub Shelby with a warm towel!" Was that why people kept yelling that word? If so, I liked it a lot. It was nearly as good as "treat" or "walk" or "good dog."

Once I was dry, April walked me back over to Teresa and we did the running again. And again.

When I was panting from all the exercise, Teresa took me back to the tent and let me sit in front of a big fan to cool off. There were other times, when we had to wait for the people to move their ladders and plat-forms and cameras around, that I'd get cold. Then Teresa would make sure I had my coat and boots on and take me to sit in front of the special light that made everything so warm.

Teresa always knew what I needed. I loved her.

I loved making her happy when I did Go-Mark or ran across the snow to April.

But sometimes I did get tired of the way humans like to do the same tricks over and over again. I liked it much better when Teresa taught me new tricks. When would she start teaching me some new tricks again?

Once I'd finished all my jobs, Teresa took me for a car ride again and then to a small room with a bed in it, a lot like the ones we'd stayed at before. It was nice because I got to sleep on the bed beside Teresa, but it wasn't really home. Home was my pack and the backyard with lizards to chase and even the strange bird in the pen who barked at me. Would we ever go back there? Or were we in this new place to stay?

We didn't go home the next day. And we didn't head up the mountain again, either. Instead, we drove through a town and got out at a quiet street. Lots of people were there, just like the day before, with their black boxes and lights and clipboards and papers and cups of coffee. Bruce and Cathryn were there, too, just watching.

Teresa did something very odd. She handed my leash to a woman who was waiting on the sidewalk! This woman seemed nice, but didn't Teresa know what a leash was for? It was supposed to keep her connected to me, so that we'd never be apart. I looked up at her and whined a bit, to remind her.

"Don't worry, Shelby," Teresa said. She bent down to rub my ears. "Just go for a walk, okay? This is an easy one. Just take a walk."

I knew she was talking to me, since she'd said my name, and her voice was calm and reassuring. So when the woman tugged gently on my leash, I followed her along the sidewalk. But I looked back at Teresa to be sure she wasn't going anywhere.

There was only a little snow here, and I wasn't the first dog to walk in it. There were footprints and yellow stains that I needed to sniff. I was busy doing this when a wonderful sound caught my ear.

Squeak!

Someone had finally remembered to take my squeaky toy out of the box! But where was it, exactly? I needed to find it!

I stood still, pulling a little against the leash, and strained my ears. There it was again! Down the block— and *up?* That was odd. How could my toy be high up in the air?

The woman seemed to know that I had something important to take care of. She dropped my leash so that I could run. I tore down the block with my ears wide open, waiting for the next squeak.

There it came! Right above me! I skidded to a stop and looked up into a tree whose bare branches spread overhead. Crouched on one of those branches was Brian—and in Brian's hand was my toy!

I jumped up to put my front paws on the tree trunk and bark up at Brian, telling him to come down with my toy. Right now!

"Cut!" someone yelled.

Brian did something even better than coming down with my toy—he dropped it. I snatched it up in midair and bit down hard, with a loud, satisfying *squeeeeeeeeeak!*

Maybe "Cut!" didn't mean anything about rubbing me with a towel after all. Maybe it meant "Give Shelby the squeaky toy!" If that was the case, I hoped the people would say it all day long.

Teresa came to take my leash as Brian climbed down. Bruce followed Teresa. "Such a good dog, Shelby!" he said to me, and put his hand down near my nose. "Can I play with the toy?" he asked me.

I could tell what he wanted, and I turned my head away while still keeping a careful eye on him. If he thought I was going to give him my squeaky toy, he was even dumber than he looked.

Bruce laughed. He didn't try to take the toy away from me, though. Good. This was not the time for a game of I've-Got-the-Toy-And-You-Don't. I could tell, just by looking up at Teresa, that we had more Training to do.

Training was more important than playing. It wasn't just that I got treats when we did Training (although of course that was nice). It was a job, and that was one of the reasons I loved it so much.

For a long time, the only job I had was filling my stomach. Now I had bowls of food every day, but even more important, I had Teresa and I had Training. I had work to do and a person to do it with. A dog needs both of those things.

Most people understood. That's why they came to watch me train and called, "Cut!" so I could get my rewards. They knew how much Training mattered.

But Bruce just wanted to play all the time. Somebody needed to explain things to him. He would probably understand better if he had some sort of job to do himself.

Days and days went by, and Teresa kept finding new places for us to do Training. Once she took me to a place a little like the beach, except that the water was not as big and did not make hills that swept up to flatten themselves on the sand. Instead, this water rushed past as if in a hurry to get somewhere. I almost thought the water wanted to play Chase-Me and that's why it was moving so fast, but I couldn't play just then. Teresa and I had a job to do.

There were people standing around, as usual. One man was by the water, wearing very tall boots that went over his knees. He seemed to be trying to play with the water just as I'd thought about doing, but he wanted to play Fetch instead of Chase-Me. He didn't quite understand how to do it right. He had a stick—that was good—but instead of throwing the stick, he just waved it at the water. A long string tied to one end of the stick flung itself a long way over the water and the man pulled it back in.

A basket sat by the man's feet, and I could smell something interesting in there. A fish! Teresa took me over to show me the basket, and the man looked down at me and smiled and kept throwing his string in the water.

Sticks are better to throw than strings, but I guessed he didn't know that.

I looked up at Teresa. What kind of Training were we going to do here?

"Okay, Shelby," Teresa told me. She pointed at the fish basket. "Pick It Up!"

So that was what we were doing here! Immediately I snatched the basket up in my teeth. That fish smelled so delicious; I was longing to eat it. But I knew that eating what I picked up was not a part of Training.

"Good girl," Teresa said. She pointed at Brian, who was standing not too far away with a box at his feet. "Put It in There!"

I trotted over to Brian and dropped the fish basket in the box. He told me I was a good dog, which I already knew, but it was nice to hear anyway. And he gave me a treat.

Then Brian picked up the basket and gave it back to the man with the stick, who put it on the ground near his feet again.

Really? After I'd just gone to all the trouble of taking the basket away?

The standing-around people gathered a little closer to the man by the river, and two of them pointed their cameras at me.

"Shelby," Teresa said to me. "Pick It Up! Put It in There!"

I knew what to do, of course.

The man with the stick was staring out across the water at his string. He did not even notice when I went up to the basket and picked it up for a second time.

I headed over to Brian.

Then the man noticed! He made a funny noise and dropped his stick. I looked back at him in surprise, the basket still in my mouth. He took a few steps toward me.

Did he want the basket back? I wasn't done with it

yet. "Put It in There!" Teresa called out, but she didn't have to say that. I already knew.

The man must have decided that if I had the basket it must be play time, because as I ran away, he flopped backward into the water to go swimming. We should have brought Hercules!

"Cut!" somebody yelled.

There was that word again, "Cut." I did not know why people kept saying it. I glanced over at Bruce, but of course, he didn't seem to know either.

I was glad when we finished playing Pick It Up. Next I got to run and race as fast as I could along the river-bank. That was great! I'd run to Teresa, who'd tell me what a good dog I was. Then I'd run to Brian, who'd tell me the same thing.

It felt so good to run, digging my claws into the mud, using all the strength in my legs, the wind rushing past my face, full of wonderful smells—trees and wet dirt and moving water, fish and squirrels and animals with stripy tails—I couldn't see any, but I could smell that they'd walked over this ground in the night. And people, of course, and treats!

"Cut!" someone yelled, and Teresa gave me a treat. Maybe that's what "Cut!" meant—"Give Shelby a treat!"

Hmmm. How could I get the people to say "Cut!" more often?

11

Another day Teresa took me to do Training by a campfire. I was interested in the campfire—it was even hotter than the special lamp in my tent, and it smelled smoky. What smelled even better, though, was the ham! Three men were sitting around the fire, talking, but the air was filled with the amazing smell of ham, which I easily detected coming from a big plastic box. The men had drinks that came in cans. A big, shiny pickup truck was parked nearby.

As usual, lots of people were standing around watching. Which job did they want to see me do today? Whatever it was, could it have something to do with that ham? It smelled marvelous—salty and meaty and delicious. I looked up at Teresa. My tail began to wag. A little drool slipped out of my mouth.

Teresa unfastened my leash. "Okay, Shelby, you can go," she said softly. She nodded at the campfire.

The men were so nice! I approached slowly, tail wagging, head down to show that I was not going to nose open that box to snatch the ham from them, but if they wanted to share I was very interested in that. They seemed to understand, because they talked to me in friendly voices and one of them pulled the ham out of the box and held it out to me.

I took it carefully from his fingers. It tasted just as good as it smelled. My tail wagged faster.

While I ate, one of the men reached over and took off my collar and looked at the tag hanging from it. What a funny thing to do! I didn't mind, though, because he gave me another bite of ham.

Then one of the men yelled.

I backed away, startled. The men were startled, too. I could tell because they all jumped up and dropped what they were holding. Two of them tried to run around the campfire and thumped into each other and fell down. None of them seemed to be thinking about me anymore.

They weren't thinking about the bag of ham, either, because they just left it lying right there in the dirt beside the campfire.

All three men raced over to the pickup truck and dove in the back. That ham was still there.

I looked over at Teresa. She nodded. "Pick It Up! Put It in There!" she called to me.

I could do Pick It Up the ham! That was *a lot* better than doing Pick It Up the fish basket!

I snatched the whole bag of ham up in my mouth. Then I pranced over to Teresa, who told me I'd been a good girl.

I wasn't sure why. I always picked up food that was on the floor. Teresa didn't usually tell me I'd been good when I did that.

Bruce and Cathryn had come to stand with Teresa. "So that was the cougar scene?" Bruce asked. "Without a cougar in it?"

"Right," Cathryn told him. "The actors just had to pretend they'd seen a cougar in the woods."

"They'll edit in shots of the cougar later, and it'll look like it was there all the time," Teresa added.

I sat patiently, that bag of ham in my mouth, wondering if anyone would mind if I sort of bit through the plastic a little. I knew how to tear open plastic and was actually pretty good at it.

"And what about your voice, when you tell Shelby what to do?" Bruce asked her. "Doesn't that get recorded?" He put out his hand and patted me on the head. But he didn't try to take the ham away from me, so maybe he was smarter than he looked.

"My voice does get recorded, but they edit it out later," Teresa told him. "Otherwise Shelby wouldn't know what to do. Okay, Shelby, drop the ham now," she said to me.

I could tell she was talking to me, but I wasn't sure what she wanted. I looked up at her, confused. She had something in her hand. She squeezed it. It squeaked.

My ears perked up and my tail swished. My toy! Teresa wiggled it enticingly. I hesitated. I wanted the toy . . . but I wanted the ham, too. To get the toy, I'd have to give up the ham.

The ham was delicious. But the toy was . . . the toy!

I opened my mouth and let the bag of ham fall to the ground so that I could snatch the toy from Teresa's hand and give it a good squeeze to make it squeak. Then I almost dropped it again so I could pick up the ham, but Teresa was too quick for me. She'd already snatched the ham up from the ground.

It was very confusing. When I had the ham in my mouth, I wanted the toy. When I had the toy, I wanted the ham.

If people were so smart they could open doors and fill bowls with dog food, why couldn't they figure out how to make a ham that squeaked?

Bruce couldn't do it, obviously, or those men around the campfire. But I was sure that some of the smart ones could make it happen if they just put their minds to it.

I got to go on a short car ride with Teresa after our visit to the campfire. Bruce and Cathryn came along, too. Cathryn rode in front with Teresa, and Bruce sat in back with me.

I didn't let him have a turn with the squeaky toy. I knew he probably wanted it, but he needed to understand that it was mine.

"Which scene is next?" Bruce asked Teresa. "I don't know how everybody keeps track, when they're shooting everything out of order."

"It's the scene where the dog digs up the deer carcass and drags it away," Teresa told him.

When we got out of the car, I knew right away which job I was going to do, because there was that big box I'd just seen at the riverside, the Put It in There box.

What would Teresa want me to work with this time? I hoped it would not be the squeaky toy. I loved Pick It Up, but I wouldn't want to Put It In There. The squeaky toy did not belong anywhere but in my mouth.

Teresa didn't understand that, however, because she took the toy away. "I'll give it back, Shelby!" she told me, laughing a little as I looked up anxiously into her face.

I forgave her. Then a buzzer sounded.

I tipped my head and looked up at Teresa. Why was the buzzer going off? That was for Dig, not for Pick It Up!

"Dig, Dig, Dig!" Teresa told me. She pointed to a spot on the ground where the dirt was loose and soft.

Oh! Now I knew just what to do. Dig wasn't just for sand or snow—it was for dirt, too. I ran to where Teresa pointed and dug as hard as I could. Gusto was not here to help, this time. The job was all mine.

My claws almost immediately scratched something strange. Not the buzzer or the treat container. I looked up at Teresa in surprise. This was not a treat! Why was I digging it up?

"Cut!" somebody yelled. And I was right—"Cut!" *did* mean "Give Shelby a treat!" because Teresa came and gave me one and told me I was a good dog for doing Dig.

I knew I was.

Bruce turned to Cathryn. "Tell me again why Shelby has to dig up the fake mule deer?"

"Because cougars bury their prey. In this scene, Shelby has been led to the deer and digs it up."

Bruce nodded, then frowned. "It's so big, though—bigger than Shelby! What's next, an elephant?"

Cathryn laughed. "Really? An elephant in the Rocky Mountains?"

"Well," Teresa said, "I'm a little worried Shelby won't understand. We've never practiced this before. But it's similar to digging up the dummy in the avalanche scene, only with dirt instead of snow. So maybe she'll get it. Right, Shelby?"

I heard my name and a question, and I wagged. If she was asking if I wanted my squeaky toy back, the answer was yes!

Then the people pointed their cameras at me again and Teresa smiled down at me. "Okay, Shelby. Pick It Up! Put It in There!"

She pointed down in the hole.

Oh! I was supposed to do Dig first and then Pick It Up whatever I'd found! Now I understood what Teresa wanted. I went back to digging, just a little more, so I could get a good look at the strange thing in the hole.

What *was* it?

It was big. Bigger than me! It had something like a long, skinny face and four limp things that stuck out like legs. There was fur on it, so it ought to have been an animal, but it didn't *smell* like an animal. It smelled like rubber. It did not smell like anything I was interested in doing Pick It Up with. I stopped digging.

I backed out of the hole. I shook my head to get dirt off my muzzle.

"Cut!" somebody yelled.

I looked over at Teresa. Treat?

Teresa shook her head and looked over at the person who'd yelled cut. "Let's try again," she said. "Ready? Okay, Shelby. Pick It Up! Put It in There!"

This was very odd. Usually I did Pick It Up with small things—toys or bones or ham. This thing was enormous! It wouldn't even *fit* in my mouth!

"Dig, Shelby! Pick It Up! Shelby, Pick It Up!"

Everyone was watching me and I felt their tension. But I wasn't sure what to do. I'd already done Dig—a little bit, anyway. And there was no buzzer and no treat, so I didn't see the point of doing Dig anymore.

I sat—doing a very good, treat-worthy Sit, I might add—and stared at them hopefully.

"Cut!"

Still no treat. People are always changing their minds about what words mean! It's one of the reasons I preferred to be a dog.

Teresa came and knelt down and took my face in her hands. I gazed at her adoringly, wagging.

"Please, let's try again. Okay, Shelby girl?"

Several times Teresa told me to Dig and Pick It Up. I tried grabbing a stick, but that was not good Pick It Up, apparently. Finally, Teresa turned to all the people who were standing around. (Why didn't *they* Pick It Up? Why did I have to do all the work?) "She needs a break," Teresa said.

Some people groaned. I was led back to the tent and took a very satisfying nap, drowsily conscious of Teresa talking to Bruce and Cathryn.

"We still have plenty of daylight left—and if we need to, we could shoot this tomorrow," Cathryn said.

"Yes, but the day of the avalanche scene we will only have a few hours. She doesn't seem interested in digging up the mule deer. They're such similar stunts, I'm worried this will happen on the mountain as well."

When I awoke, we went back to do more of the same. I decided to try digging a little more, see if that made everyone happy. I scratched up the dirt so that more of that strange, rubbery object poked out of the hole. Teresa gave me a treat! Yes!

"Good job, Shelby! Now Put It in There!"

I edged back into the shallow hole. Gingerly I took one of the leg-things between my teeth and tried tugging a little. It wouldn't budge.

I dropped it and backed away. Surely we could do a different job now? How about Go Mark?

"Cut!" the same person yelled. Again, nobody gave me a treat.

"Shelby," Teresa said in the voice she used for Training. "Pick It Up! Put It in There!"

Well, if I had to. . . .

I went back to the hole and took the strange object in my mouth by what ought to have been the neck. I tried to Pick It Up.

It was heavy! I'd never be able to get it off the ground. And it tasted so strange!

"Pick It Up!" I heard Teresa call.

I gripped hard with my teeth and braced my feet in the soft dirt of the hole and dragged. It took all my strength! The muscles in my neck trembled. I took one step backward, then another. Finally, I had the thing out of the hole. At least some of it. What would have been the head if it had been a real animal was out, but the rear end and legs were still in the hole.

I dropped it and looked up at Teresa. That must be enough.

"Cut!" the person shouted.

"Good dog, Shelby. Good dog!" Bruce told me. "You got it halfway there. You can do it! Good girl!"

He was very enthusiastic. If he thought this was so exciting, why didn't he come and help me Pick It Up this strange, heavy thing?

And why wasn't Teresa giving me a treat?

"Let's go again," Teresa said. "Ready? Shelby, Pick It Up! Put It in There!"

She pointed at the box.

I sat down. I'd gotten the weird thing out of the hole. That should be enough.

"Shelby," Teresa said again. Her voice was not stern. It had so much love in it that my tail started to stir, even though I didn't like this job. "Pick It Up! Put It in There!"

I looked up at Teresa. She smiled at me.

Teresa wanted me to do Pick It Up. She wanted me to do it because she loved me and this was our job, the one that we did together.

I loved Teresa, too. If she asked me, I'd do it.

Even though I'd rather go back to the campfire and do Training with the ham some more.

I lowered my head and gripped the rubbery thing by its leg. Slowly I backed across the ground toward the box. The thing resisted me, almost as if it were playing Tug-on-a-Stick. But Tug-on-a-Stick was fun, and this was *not*.

Still, I kept going. Step by step I got closer to the box. Everybody was watching me. Cathryn had her hands clasped tightly in front of her. Teresa was nodding at me and smiling, but I knew I wasn't done yet.

At last I got the strange object over right next to the box. There was no way I could get it up high enough to go *in* the box, so this would just have to do.

"Cut!" somebody yelled.

"Good dog, Shelby!" Teresa called out. "Good girl!"

She came right over and gave me a *handful* of treats. But even better, she bent down and hugged me and rubbed her face on the top of my head.

Bruce and Cathryn patted me, too, and so did a lot of the standing-around people. I still didn't understand why they hadn't helped if they'd wanted that thing in the box so much. But I didn't really mind.

I was a good dog. I was Teresa's dog.

That was enough.

12

A few days later, Teresa took me to a parking lot and I met a new dog pack! Instead of Luke and Bode and Hercules and Angel, there were three new dogs I had never met—a big shaggy one, a large muscular one with short, sleek fur, and funny teeth, and a small one with wiry hair that went every which way. She was as small as Angel!

Teresa let us meet each other and sniff. They all smelled fine, although Shaggy Male wanted me to know he was in charge. He put his head up higher than mine and kept his eyes on me.

I didn't mind if he wanted to be in charge right now. I lowered my head to let him know that I was okay with that—for the moment.

Things might change later.

That was a strange and silly day! At home Teresa would be frustrated if Bode or Luke or Hercules knocked over the trash can. (Angel tried sometimes, but she was too little to move the can even if she tried.)

Teresa didn't even allow *me* to knock over the trash can at home, and I was her most special dog. (Why do people put things in the garbage that smell so good if they don't want dogs to knock it over?)

But here in the parking lot, the big male dog with the short fur kept knocking over a tall plastic trash can, and Teresa never even told him no! Trash spilled out every time, most of it crumpled pieces of paper. Hidden among the paper were tiny treats that tasted like chicken, and my new pack and I were allowed to get them all!

We pawed at the paper and shoved it aside with our muzzles and gobbled up the treats. I was the fastest. I'd had lots of practice at digging through trash and finding the tasty things hidden inside it.

Shaggy Male did not like that I could eat so many treats in such a short time. When my muzzle came close to his as we both burrowed after the same treat, he lifted his lip and growled at me.

I ignored him. He wasn't in charge now! I snatched up the treat and got it.

"That's enough," Teresa said firmly.

"Cut!" someone yelled, and Teresa called to me to come to her, so I did. She snapped my collar around my neck with my leash attached to it.

"I don't like the way that other dog's acting around Shelby," she said, pointing to Shaggy Male. "I can't risk her safety."

I looked up to see if she was talking to me—her voice said, "Cut that out!" Maybe it was bad to be getting things out of the trash after all? But I wasn't the one who'd knocked the can over!

To my relief I saw that Teresa was not talking to me. She was directing her words at another person, one with a clipboard.

The man nodded, and that was the last time we were allowed to eat chicken treats out of the trash can. Maybe "Cut!" meant "No more treats from the trash." If that was true, I didn't like "Cut!" as much as I used to.

In the evening, that Angel-sized dog stood in front of a house and spun in a circle, while I stood and watched. She was given treats, even though it was so much easier than Dig It Up and Put It in There that it hardly even counted as a trick.

Late one afternoon, Teresa and I went on to another house. The new dog pack didn't get to come. They were just not as good at hard tricks as I was. I lay down next to Teresa in the car and put my head in her lap to show her that I understood I was her best dog.

At the house, I met an old friend—Gusto! He came out of the door to meet me and we ran around the yard before coming together to sniff faces and under each other's tails. I pranced away and put my front legs low on the ground with my rear end up high, tail wagging, to invite Gusto to play, but he turned his head and looked toward April. I saw that Gusto was doing Training with April and had no time for play.

I understood these kinds of things better than Bruce did.

Teresa and April took me and Gusto inside the house, and there we met two nice men. They called each other Gavin and Taylor. I liked Taylor the best. His hands smelled particularly good—he'd been eating a turkey and cheese sandwich when we arrived.

Teresa handed my leash to Taylor, and April gave Gusto's leash to Gavin. "Okay, time for a walk!" Teresa told us.

"Walk"? I knew that word. It was a good word! My tail wagged happily.

Gavin and Taylor walked Gusto and me out of the front door. The watching people were all around, as usual; I noticed Bruce and Cathryn were there, too.

I glanced at Bruce, hoping he'd figure out that Gusto and I were doing Training now. This was serious work.

Gavin and Taylor may have been nice, but they didn't know the first thing about taking a dog for a walk! Once we got to the front yard, they turned around and took us right back inside! "Cut!" somebody yelled.

Did "Cut!" mean "Take the dogs for a very short walk!"?

Gavin and Taylor took us for a lot of walks, but they never got it right. We always went right back inside as soon as we reached the front yard. They were as dumb as Bruce.

"This is the scene after the avalanche," I heard Cathryn say to Bruce on one of our trips back inside the house. "When Gavin and Taylor take the dogs off the mountain and bring them to the house."

"But we haven't even filmed the avalanche yet," Bruce said, shaking his head. "It's impossible to keep all the scenes straight!"

"Good thing you're just a screenwriter and not the director, then," Cathryn told him. "Remember what he told us? The avalanche is going to be the last thing they shoot."

"Good thing you're a director and I'm not. I'd rather just play with the dogs."

"Well, next movie I direct, I'll make sure there are dogs, so you'll have something to do."

"The avalanche is Shelby's big day," Bruce said. "I hope she can do it."

"Oh, Bruce," Cathryn said, "she *has* to do it."

Going for very short walks with Gavin and Taylor was a pretty boring job, so I was glad when that was over. What happened the next day, however, was not boring at all.

Teresa and I drove to a park, like the one where I'd met Lucas. Lucas wasn't here this time, though. Instead, there was a family—a mother and father, two kids big enough to slide down slides and swing on swings, and a baby sitting on the mother's lap.

I got to say hi to them all quickly. The older kids talked to me and petted me gently, but the baby just stared at me with very wide eyes. I licked at her bare toes; they tasted excellent, almost sweet. She squealed with surprise, and I looked back at her with equal surprise. I'd never heard a human make a sound like that before!

Then Teresa called me over. The family sat at a picnic table and didn't pay any more attention to me—except the baby. She never took her eyes off me.

Brian was there, too. He put a big piece of steak on a grill near the picnic table. I was as interested in that steak as the baby was in me! How odd that none of the family paid any attention to it. They were talking to each other and looking in the other direction. Why would anyone ignore a steak?

"Okay, Shelby," Teresa told me. She pointed to the steak. "Pick It Up!"

Excellent! I would be very happy to Pick It Up the steak.

I raced to the grill, grabbed the steak by a corner, and snatched it. None of the family was watching, except the baby! She squealed again with surprise and made funny sounds that were not words, but no one paid attention to her, any more than they did to me.

I took the steak right to Teresa, and she had my squeaky toy ready in her hand. A little reluctantly, I dropped the steak and took the toy. The toy was good, of course—but why did I have to give up the steak when I'd just done such a good job of Pick It Up?

Then Teresa took me (I took my squeaky toy) to another part of the park. There were trees and rocks here, no picnic tables or playgrounds. There, she lay down on the ground. What fun! I loved it when Teresa got down to my level.

I lay down with her and rolled over so that she could scratch my belly. She scratched better than anyone. I didn't even mind when she took the squeaky toy away and handed it to April.

April handed Teresa something, and I sat bolt upright, excitement quivering all through my body. It was the steak!

Teresa put the steak on the ground and gripped one end of it between her fingers. The other end of the steak was mine! I got to tear off big chunks and gulp them down. Steak is delicious! Even better than ham.

"There isn't a scene in the movie where the dog gets to eat steak with a person," I heard Bruce say to Cathryn.

"No, this is the scene where the dog and Big Kitten share the steak," Cathryn told him. "Obviously they're not going to put Shelby right next to a young cougar, so Teresa's filling in for her. They'll paint in Big Kitten later, and it'll look like the dog and the cougar are in the same scene."

I didn't know what they were talking about. Why were they mentioning kittens when there weren't any kittens here? But it didn't matter. What mattered was the steak. I finished it up and licked Teresa all over her face as the person yelled, "Cut!"

I didn't even try to figure out what "Cut!" meant this time. I was beginning to think that the humans didn't understand that word any more than I did.

I guessed that Teresa had enjoyed the job with the steak as much as I did, because our next job involved food, too. We went to a house with a car in the driveway and a bag of groceries sitting in the car.

Teresa had brought the big Put It in There box, so I knew what was coming. But we had to wait a little, while all the watching people got ready to see me work. Bruce came over to talk to Teresa while everyone got in place. "This is going to be a fun scene," he said to Teresa. "I can't wait to see her carry off the bag of groceries. Every dog who sees this movie will be inspired!"

Teresa smiled. "Let's just hope she doesn't run off with my groceries when I get her home," she told him. "Okay, Shelby, it's time. Pick It Up! Put It in There!"

I ran to the car, jumped up, and seized the bag. To be honest, I would have done that even if Teresa hadn't told me to. It smelled wonderful. There were tangy oranges in there and a bunch of carrots and apples. Those were not too interesting to me, but I loved the smell of a long, skinny loaf of bread. There was some bacon in a package, too! Bacon *and* steak in one day?

I grabbed a corner of the bag in my mouth and gave it a good shake. That's what I often did to things I picked up, just as I did to my squeaky toy. It always seemed like the right thing to do.

The bag ripped. Everything inside tumbled to the ground. Oranges and apples rolled down the driveway. The bread flew through the air and plopped onto the grass. I pounced on the bacon and Teresa ran over to pull it from my mouth as somebody yelled, "Cut!"

That again?

I looked up at Teresa with the bacon in her hand. I wagged hopefully. She'd let me have the steak earlier. Would I get the bacon, too?

"Shelby, that's not it," Teresa told me. She was trying to look stern, but her mouth was twitching. Some of the watching people were chuckling.

"Going again!" someone called out, and people came to collect the groceries and put them in a new bag. I went to the side to stand and wait with Teresa.

"Okay, Shelby, do it right," Teresa told me. "Pick It Up! Put It in There!"

I ran for the groceries again, got the bag in my teeth, and shook it, just like last time. Then I chased the apples all the way down the driveway to where they met the street. It was like Fetch! It was great!

This time some of the watching people groaned. Bruce didn't, though. He was laughing so hard that he

was holding on to Cathryn's shoulder to keep from falling over.

I thought we were having fun, too. People came running to get the rest of the apples and I picked up one in my mouth in case anybody wanted to throw it for me.

"Teresa, can't you make her be serious?" someone called out.

"She's a dog," Bruce said, getting his breath back. "They don't do *serious*."

Teresa came to take the apple from me. I looked up at her wagging. Did I get a treat? I did Pick It Up, didn't I? Okay, I didn't do Put It in There, but how was I supposed to when everything fell out of the bag?

No treat. Really?

We played Rip-the-Bag a few times, and Bruce kept laughing, but I never got a treat. Apparently Teresa really wanted me to do Put It in There, even though Rip-the-Bag was a lot more fun.

Okay. If that's what Teresa wanted. The next time, I got the bag in my teeth and *didn't* shake it. If I was going to finish Pick It Up! Put It in There! that was what I needed to do.

Teresa was waiting by the box. I pulled the bag of bruised apples and leaky oranges and squashed bread over to her, lifted it up as high as I could, and dumped it in the box.

Could Teresa and I share that bacon now?

Apparently not. But I did get my treat and a lot of praise from Teresa. Bruce and Cathryn came over to tell me I was a good dog, too.

"One more day of filming and we're all done, Shelby! Bet you'll be glad to go home!" Bruce said.

I licked Bruce's hand to show him that I liked him, even though he was not too bright. At least he understood that Rip-the-Bag was fun.

"Okay, that's it for today," Teresa told me, clipping my leash onto my collar. "Back up on the mountain tomorrow, Shelby."

"The avalanche?" Bruce asked.

"That's right. Shelby's big scene."

"She'll do it," Bruce said confidently. He reached down to scratch my back, and I wiggled happily. "She's done great."

"Well, it's all for nothing if we don't get the last scene," Teresa said. "We can't do a lot of takes of the avalanche scene like we just did here. It's too complicated to set up. We won't get that many chances."

13

In the morning, Teresa and I drove back up the snowy mountain. When we stopped and got out of the car, there were lots and lots of people standing around a big field of deep snow.

Bruce and Cathryn came over to see me, but neither of them had treats. "This is your big day, Shelby," Bruce said.

"First you dig yourself out of the avalanche, and then you dig up the dummy," Cathryn added. I heard the word "dig," but it wasn't a command. People are like that—they'll says words like "sit" and "down," but it won't be a command for a dog and doing Sit or Down won't earn any treats.

Teresa had my coat and boots all ready for me. I was

used to the boots now and didn't try to shake them off. She took me to a new, cozy room with wooden walls. It was just the right size for me. Snow had been heaped over it.

Teresa showed me a ramp that led up to a hole in the roof. She let me go up the ramp so that I could put my head out and see what was up there.

Nothing that interesting. Just all the people who usually came to watch me do my jobs.

Then I went back down the ramp and Teresa took off my leash and coat and boots. She told me I was a good dog. "This is the last day, Shelby," she said. "You can do it. I know you can."

Then she left me inside the room alone.

From the outside, someone laid a cover over the hole in the roof. It was a piece of white cloth that looked a lot like the snow.

This seemed very odd. I thought I'd had a job to do—but I never did jobs all alone in a room. Teresa was always with me. People were always watching to see what a good dog I was.

Here there was nobody to see me.

I yawned. This room was cozy, even if it didn't have a heat lamp like the tent. I curled up and put my tail over my nose. It was nice of the people to give me such a good place for a nap while I waited for my next job with Teresa.

I could hear voices outside. One of them belonged to Bruce. "How will Shelby get out of there?" he asked. "With all that snow over the top?"

"From our view, it looks like the box is completely covered, but it's not really," Cathryn told him. "Shelby can actually just jump out of the hole with no problem. But in the movie, it will look like she's been buried by the avalanche and dug herself out."

I wagged sleepily that they were saying my name.

"Ready, Teresa?" someone else called out. I wagged again, for Teresa's name.

"Shelby! Come!" Teresa called.

My ears perked up. Teresa wanted me.

But it was so nice and comfortable in here. Did I really have to? I sniffed. I could smell treats outside. Teresa would probably give me one if I went out.

But . . . I wasn't really that hungry. I didn't really need another treat, not right now. Not as much as I wanted a nap.

My eyes slowly closed.

"Come on, Shelby!" Bruce called.

Cathryn added her voice. "Shelby! Sweetie! Come out!"

They probably wanted me to play. I didn't feel like playing.

"Cut!" someone called out. But nobody came to give me a treat or rub me with a towel or take me for a walk—even a short one. I wished the people would figure out what they meant by "Cut!" or stop yelling it.

There was a rustle up above me. The piece of cloth covering the hole in the roof had moved aside and Teresa's face was looking in.

I wagged. It was nice to see her. Maybe she'd come down and we could take a nap together. Sometimes we did that on the couch back home.

Teresa had something in her hand. My head lifted up at the smell.

"Shelby, want some steak?" Teresa called down to me.

A wonderful, meaty smell filled the little room. I got up and shook myself from head to tail and trotted up the ramp to take the morsel of steak from Teresa's hand. I wasn't hungry, but if she was offering it to me, it was only polite to accept.

"We need this shot!" someone outside called out. "We're running out of time!"

"Come out and you'll get more steak," Teresa told me.

I didn't know what she was saying, but I sure appreciated the treat. I licked her fingers to get the last of the meaty taste from them. Then she pulled away and put the piece of cloth back over the opening.

Okay. I guessed we were done. I headed back down the ramp and curled up on the floor again. Now I was more full than ever. Definitely time for a nap.

Brian and April called my name. I yawned. Why didn't they come inside my cozy room if they wanted to see me?

"Shelby! Come!" Teresa called.

I felt a little guilty. I knew I was supposed to come when Teresa wanted me. But it was so nice and warm in here. . . .

"Come on, Shelby! Come on!" Lots of people seemed to be saying my name now.

I rolled over onto my side and stretched out. I groaned with contentment. I'd been working so hard, doing Training every day. Couldn't I have a little time just to sleep?

"If we don't hurry up, we're not going to get the last shot of the day!" I heard somebody yell.

"What's he talking about?" That was Bruce.

I heard a new voice answering him. "This is the last day we have a permit for shooting up here on the mountain. We have to get this shot of her escaping, and then the one of her digging up the dummy. If we don't get both scenes wrapped today, we won't be able to have the avalanche scene in the movie at all."

"We could just get a new permit, right?"

"That would take a long time. The snow would all be melted."

"But without the avalanche scene, the movie makes no sense! We have to get this!"

"I know, Bruce."

"She can do this; I know she can." That was Teresa.

"Shelby!" Bruce called out. "Please! Focus!"

It was probably best to pay no attention to Bruce.

"Oh, thanks, April," I heard Teresa say. "This will work if anything will. Okay, I need quiet, everybody. Shelby! Come! Come on, girl!"

I sat bolt upright. What was that sound?

Something squeaked! Teresa was playing with my squeaky toy!

Without me!

I couldn't let that happen. I jumped to my feet, all sleepiness gone, and tore up the ramp. That piece of cloth was in the way, but I shoved it with my head, and it moved. It was heavier than I expected, though. There was snow piled up on it.

On the other side of that snow there was my squeaky toy *and* Teresa! I pushed my snout at the cloth, pawing at it.

The cloth gave way. I got my upper body out of the hole and clawed my way into the light. Snow flew. I struggled all the way out and tore down a slope of snow toward Teresa, who was kneeling with a piece of steak in one hand and my squeaky toy in the other and a big smile on her face.

I grabbed the toy, shook it hard, dropped it on the snow, snapped up the bit of steak, and seized my

squeaky toy again. Everybody clapped and cheered. Lots of people petted me—Bruce included. He probably wanted a turn with my squeaky toy, but I didn't give it to him.

I could tell I'd been a very good dog.

"Perfect! We got the shot we needed!" someone yelled. "All right, moving on to the last shot!"

Teresa was petting me, but she was looking at the sky. "That took most of the day. We're losing light," she said, and her voice was tense. "We have to get everybody off the mountain soon for safety reasons. We can't ask the whole crew to ride down in the dark."

"Hurry!" someone yelled.

I felt the tension in Teresa—it came down her arms and into her hands as they stroked me. Clearly, the person who yelled had upset her. I stared up into her eyes and tried to let her know that whatever was going on, I was a good dog who would do her best to help.

14

I could sense from the way the light was changing that it would soon be time for us to all leave and go back down to where we would sleep and eat dinner. But unlike every other day, when people were relaxed and laughing as they put things in the backs of trucks, today people were running back and forth, carrying things and peering at their black boxes. The only person not doing anything, as usual, was Bruce, but even he seemed worried.

I heard a door slam and saw Brian with Gusto on a leash. Each of them had on a coat and boots.

I dragged Teresa over to exchange greetings. Would we play Dig? Or Take a Short Walk? I hoped it was Dig. That was much more fun.

All of the people continued to mill around urgently, while Gusto and I sniffed. Bruce and Cathryn stood with Teresa and Brian, and eventually we all walked right up to the edge of a fresh field of snow, higher up the mountain than the place where my warm little nap room was buried. Unlike around the tents where so many people had been walking, there was not a single footprint to be seen.

"Gusto first. Then Shelby," Teresa told Brian. He nodded.

"Gusto, Dig!" Brian said. He unsnapped Gusto's leash.

Gusto bounded out onto the snow and sniffed hard, sticking his nose into the fluffy white stuff. Then he began to do Dig. I looked up at Teresa anxiously. Gusto was going to get all the treats!

I heard the buzzer make its noise under the snow. My ears perked up.

"Shelby, Dig!" Teresa told me. She unsnapped my leash, too.

I jumped into the deep snow and it fountained up around my feet. Usually snow was a lot of fun, but here I couldn't enjoy it, because I was not sure what to do.

Gusto was digging for treats. I should do Dig with him and get my share.

But the buzzer was going off under the snow far

away from Gusto! Should I do Dig where the buzzer was? Should I do Dig with Gusto?

I didn't like this feeling. When Teresa and I did Training, I usually knew just what she wanted. Now I didn't know.

"I can't hear the buzzer," Bruce said. "Isn't that weird?"

"No, it's buried pretty deep in the snow," Teresa said. "I'm not surprised that we can't hear it. But Shelby should be able to. Shelby! Dig! Dig! Dig!" she called out.

I *knew* Dig. I was supposed to do Dig. But where?

Feeling a little panicked, I ran in a big circle around Gusto. He didn't look up at me. He was busy with his job. I wanted to be busy, too, but I didn't know how.

Gusto got to the treats at the bottom of his hole and gobbled them up. Brian called to him and he came. I figured that's what I should do, too, and I returned to Teresa and wagged hopefully. Had I done it right? Would I get a treat?

"Try again!" one of the watching people called out.

Teresa sighed. "It's okay, Shelby. Good girl, Shelby. We'll do it again," she told me.

People hurried out to brush at the snow with brooms and scrape at it with rakes until it was unmarked again.

Then we did the trick again. But I still didn't under-

stand! Gusto dug in the same spot, but the buzzer still rang somewhere else.

"Dig Dig Dig!" I heard Teresa call.

Okay! I would do Dig! I would do what Teresa wanted! I ran to where the buzzer was going off under the snow and dug there, as fast as I could.

"Cut!" someone yelled out. "Teresa, why's she digging way over there? She's supposed to be with the other dog!"

"I don't know!" Teresa called back. "Shelby, Come!"

Why was she calling me to come to her before I'd dug up the buzzer? I ran over to see if I'd get a treat, but I didn't.

Unfair! I'd done Dig where the buzzer was. That was the job!

Teresa knelt and held my head in her hands and gazed into my eyes. Her voice was warm and kind. "I know you don't understand this, Shelby girl, but we only have a little time left and then all this work we have done together won't count for a thing. Just go to the buzzer and Dig, okay? I know you can do it."

The next time I didn't do Dig at the buzzer, since that hadn't generated much enthusiasm. I ran up to Gusto, but that buzzer was still bothering me. So I ran away from Gusto and rolled in the snow.

People groaned. Teresa called me, and I came. No treat, though.

This was not as fun as Training usually was.

I could tell Teresa didn't think it was fun, either. She still spoke to me softly and called me a good girl. "Just try again, Shelby. You can do it," she told me. "I know you're trying."

But beneath her kind voice, I could sense frustration. I could feel it and smell it in the other people, too. They were worried.

What had happened? Why was Training suddenly so confusing and difficult? I didn't like it. Maybe we should go back into town and play Knock-Over-the-Trash-Can or Rip-the-Bag some more.

"One more time," Teresa said with a sigh. Gusto bounded out into the snow, sniffed, and began to do Dig.

The buzzer sounded in its strange, faraway place.

I sat down in the snow and looked up at Teresa. I wanted to do what Teresa wanted. I knew that would make her happy. I just couldn't figure out what it was.

People were looking at their wrists and then frowning at the sky.

"We're going to have to call the day pretty soon," Cathryn told Bruce. "The sun is nearly down."

"Hey, wait!" someone called, far away from our group. It was April. "I can hear the buzzer! It's over *here*! No wonder Shelby's confused!"

Teresa groaned. "You're kidding! Shelby, don't worry. Shelby, good girl," she told me, and bent down to stroke my head and scratch behind my ears. Suddenly, she was relaxed, which let me relax, too. I licked her nose.

There was a lot of running around and talking after that, but nobody told me or Gusto to do Dig. Teresa put on my coat and boots, and Brian did the same for Gusto. I'd figured out that I never did a job while I had my coat on; coats and boots on dogs meant it was time for the people to work. So we waited.

"The signal was going to the wrong buzzer!" somebody called out after a while. "All fixed now."

"Are you sure?" Teresa called out. "I don't want Shelby getting any more upset."

"Yes, sure!" the person said.

More people hurried out to broom the snow around and Teresa talked to me as she took off my coat and boots. "You were trying, weren't you, Shelby girl? I'm so sorry we messed up. Now we've got it right. It'll be okay this time."

"All right, everyone!" a man called out. "This is the last take."

Everyone went very still. A few of them were shaking their heads. Then Teresa spoke.

"I know how hard everyone has worked to get here, and I'm sorry if it's all for nothing. Let's just do our jobs and hope that Shelby does hers."

Every single person turned to look at me. I wagged a little nervously. What was going on?

"Shelby, you're so sweet," Teresa said fondly, rubbing behind my ears. "Guys, we have to talk about something else. She's picking up on our anxiety, and that won't help her perform."

People turned away. Teresa held my collar. "Go, Gusto!" Once more Gusto bounded out, sniffed, and pawed furiously at the snow.

I quivered with eagerness and anxiety, too. I wanted to do Dig right. I wanted praise and a treat and for Teresa not to be worried anymore. But I hadn't been able to do it right yet. What if I got it wrong again?

"Shelby, Dig!" Teresa told me, releasing her hold.

The buzzer sounded. But now it was in the right place, just where Gusto was clawing at the snow. I knew what to do! I leaped forward, bounding through the snow, and plowed right into the hole that Gusto was making. That was okay, though. He dug and I dug and snow was flung into the air and we got closer and closer to the buzzer and the treats.

Then, suddenly, two men came lumbering across the snow, running clumsily in big, heavy boots. They threw themselves down next to me and Gusto and started to do Dig, too, scooping at the snow with mittened hands.

I backed away. Usually just Gusto and I did Dig! Did these people want treats, too?

I knew I was not supposed to eat food that belonged to people. Teresa had made that clear to me. Food on the floor was for dogs. Food on tables and plates was for people.

Maybe these people didn't know the rules, though. Maybe they didn't understand that the treats down in the snow were for dogs. Maybe they were so hungry they didn't care.

I remembered being hungry like that, when I was younger. Should I let the men have the treats? I looked over at Teresa.

"Shelby, Dig! Get in there!" Teresa called out.

"Dig Dig Dig!" Bruce echoed.

Well, okay. If Teresa wanted me to do Dig, I would. But I hoped I wouldn't get in trouble for taking treats away from hungry humans!

All four of us—me, Gusto, and the two strange people—dug and dug at the snow. Then something new happened that made me pull my nose out of the snow in surprise.

We were getting close to the treats; I could smell that. But my claws had scraped something strange. It was a person! A person in a puffy coat with a hat on his head, buried under the snow with the treats and the buzzer!

But it was not a real person, not at all. It did not move and it did not smell alive. It smelled fake and rubbery, kind of like that strange object I'd had to Pick It Up and Put It in There a few days ago.

The treats were under this not-person, so I snatched up my share and backed away just as someone called out, "Cut!" The men sat back on their heels, grinning. They did not seem to want any treats after all. So why had they been digging?

But I had a bigger worry at the moment. I looked over at Teresa in concern. She wasn't going to tell me to Pick It Up this person and Put It in There, was she? It was even bigger than the furry thing with legs had been!

Teresa did not say, "Shelby, Pick It Up!" Thank goodness! Instead, she called me and I got a whole handful of treats and lots of praise.

"That's a wrap, everyone!" someone called out.

"You did it, Shelby!"

"Good girl!"

People were smiling and laughing. Lots of them came over to praise me, including the men who'd helped us do Dig. I knew I was a good girl; I could already tell from how happy Teresa was. But I always liked to hear it.

"I don't even know why they use a buzzer anyway," Bruce said while he petted me. "Why not a doorbell?

My dog Tucker always barks when he hears a door-bell."

Nobody answered him. People often had more serious jobs to do than answer Bruce.

"Shelby was perfect," Cathryn says. "We got the shot."

"Shelby," Bruce said. "You saved the movie!" He held down his hand and he had a piece of Teresa's steak in his palm. I gently took it from him.

This time, I decided, it did make sense to pay attention to Bruce.

I'd been such a good dog that I got to go for a long car ride with Teresa the next day. At first Teresa let me have my squeaky toy, but after I'd curled up on the backseat with it and given it a thorough chewing, Teresa stopped the car and leaned over the seat to take the toy away from me.

"Sorry, Shelby, but there's no way I can listen to that all the way home," she said.

We drove and drove and drove. I took a long nap, and when I woke up, the air that poured in through the open window of the car was warmer.

Soon I could lean against the window and sniff hard and pick up smells that I recognized. The car turned a corner and I knew my nose had been right. We were back where we'd started! We were at Teresa's house!

Teresa let me out of the car and I raced around her front yard in circles before running to the gate that led to the back. I could hear my pack welcoming both of us. Bode and Luke, Hercules and Angel, were all barking their happiness on the other side of the fence.

When Teresa opened the gate, I charged inside. My pack sniffed me all over, learning from me where I'd been and what I'd been eating and how many other people and dogs I'd met. I sniffed them, too, led us all in a race around the pool, and returned to Teresa, panting with happiness. I wagged and looked at Teresa, busy hugging Hercules and stroking Luke's back and scratching Bode's neck and making sure little Angel was not being forgotten.

This was the first time I'd ever come back to a place I'd left. When I'd gone away from the yard where I'd been born, I'd never seen it again. When I'd left the place of plastic bags or the building with pens and dogs and Megan, I'd never returned.

But I'd come back to Teresa's house.

The place of plastic bags had been a lonely place. Even when my stomach had been full—which wasn't often!—I'd had no sister to stay warm with, no pack to play with, and no person to love.

Then Megan had come to be my first person, and she'd taken me to my pen with bowls of food and a roof overhead. There I wasn't hungry or lonely anymore. That had been a good place. But it wasn't a home.

I hadn't understood that then. But I knew it now.

My home was here, where I had a person and a pack and a job to do. Even when Teresa and I left to do Training in other places, we would always come back here.

That was such a marvelous idea, I had to chase a lizard out of sheer joy. It scuttled away under a rock. Lizards never understood that their job was to be caught.

But I did *my* jobs well.

I thought back to all the jobs I'd done—digging with Gusto in the snow, doing Pick It Up the bag of groceries, running up the ramp so that I could jump out of the hole and get my squeaky toy from Teresa, finding my mark over and over again. Being a good dog and making all those people so happy.

I'd loved doing all those jobs. Well, except dragging that big, heavy, rubbery long-legged thing out of the hole in the ground. But even that had been worth it, to please Teresa.

And now that all my work was done, I got to come back home. I'd never been so happy. The only thing that would have made it better was my squeaky toy to chew.

And some of my new friends to see. It was great to

be back, but what about Gusto? What about Brian and April and my other human friends? Even Bruce. Would they ever come to see me again? Would they watch me do my jobs and be a good dog?

I hoped so.

But long days went by, and they didn't come. I wasn't sad, though. I was busy playing with my pack and chasing lizards and making sure Teresa stayed close to me. Also, I had to watch that bird in a cage. A lot.

So I didn't have too much time to miss my friends.

Then a day came when Teresa gave me a bath and brushed my fur until it was glossy and smooth. I didn't like getting wet, but I loved the extra attention and the feel of the brush in my fur. It was almost worth the water and the dreadful taste of the soap and the way I didn't smell like myself afterward.

"You have to look your best. We're going to the premiere of *A Dog's Way Home*," Teresa told me.

I recognized a few of the words in that sentence— "*Dog's*" and "*Home*." I licked her nose. Yes, I was a dog. Yes, I was home. I didn't know why she needed to tell me that, but I was happy to hear her voice anytime she felt like talking to me.

Then I got to go for a car ride with Teresa! Just her and me, of course. The way it ought to be.

When she stopped the car and we got out, we were in a very strange place.

It wasn't home, with the backyard and the pool and the lizards and my pack.

It wasn't a snowy mountain, either.

It was a place with a soft rug on the sidewalk. I sniffed at it. Lots of people had been walking on it. More were standing around the rug, talking loudly and smiling. Some were holding small black boxes up in front of their faces. The boxes made flashes of light.

"Bella! Bella!" the people called.

I was glad Teresa and I were connected with our leash. It was all very strange.

We walked together down the carpet and into a big building. And there, inside the building, were all my old friends!

I saw Bruce and Cathryn! I saw Brian! Next to Brian was April, and April was holding a leash with Gusto on the other end!

I ran to them, greeting Gusto first. He licked my cheek and I licked his ear. Then I hurried to April and Brian, Bruce and Cathryn, my tail wagging so hard it swatted them on their knees and legs.

Everybody petted me and talked to me and to Teresa and each other. I sat down and looked at Gusto with expectation.

When were we going to Dig? When I was with

Gusto, we always did Dig. And all these people had come to watch us! It was going to be so much fun!

But the people seemed to have forgotten about Dig. Instead of taking us somewhere there was sand or snow or dirt, they took us into a dark room with many, many chairs.

The people sat down in the chairs. Gusto and I sat together on the floor. After a little bit, the room went dark. Some lights flickered and moved on a big wall, but I could not smell them, so they weren't very interesting.

Gusto and I curled up together on the floor. I put my head on my paws and shut my eyes. Since the room was dark, it was probably time for a cozy nap.

Even if we weren't going to do Dig, I was glad to be here with Gusto and Teresa and my other friends. I was glad that there were so many interesting things for me to do with Teresa, and so many people to watch me be a good dog.

And I was glad that, when this was over, I had a home to go back to, a home with a dog pack and lizards and food in bowls and a roof to keep the rain away.

I loved all of those things. I loved all of my friends, especially Teresa.

Together Teresa and I had been in rooms with beds and parks and up on the side of a mountain. We'd gone to a beach and the bank of a river and a place

where a campfire burned and men sat beside it, shar-
ing ham.

I couldn't wait to find out where Teresa and I would
go next. As long as we were together, it would be
marvelous.

Shelby's Movie Star Biography

Shelby's first big break in the movie business was her starring role as Bella in *A Dog's Way Home*. In the movie, Bella is separated from her owner, Lucas, and sets off on a journey to find him. She travels over snowy mountains and through city streets, scavenging food where she can find it. Along the way she meets up with an orphaned cougar she calls Big Kitten, helps to rescue a skier from an avalanche, joins a pack of loose dogs, and always remains true to her purpose of finding Lucas again.

Shelby's own life story is nearly as adventurous as Bella's. As a young dog, she lived as a stray and was found scavenging food from a landfill. Rescued by an animal control officer named Megan, she was taken to a county shelter. While waiting for adoption she met Bruce Cameron and his wife, Cathryn Michon. Bruce is the author of the novel *A Dog's Way Home*, and

Bruce and Cathryn cowrote the screenplay that transformed the book into a movie.

Bruce was delighted to meet Shelby, who looked exactly like the photograph of Bella on the cover of *A Dog's Way Home*. But Shelby was a stray who had never had even the most basic training. Could she really learn to do all of the things a movie dog needs to know?

Shelby could! With the help of her trainer, Teresa, Shelby mastered all of the skills she'd need to portray Bella on the screen. Along with her fellow actors, Ashley Judd, Edward James Olmos, Alexandra Shipp, and Jonah Hauer-King, she delighted audiences with her performance as a loving dog who risks everything to find her owner once more.

After her star turn as Bella, Shelby moved on to a new challenge. She is being trained to act as a comfort dog, visiting children who are in hospitals and helping to cheer them up. If a sequel to *A Dog's Way Home* is ever made, however, Shelby will be back at work on the movie set with her friends!

Shelby's Story is based on Bella's life, but it is fiction. Not every episode in the book is true to life. But Shelby did get rescued from life in a landfill, did learn to be a movie star, and is as loyal and loving in real life as she is in this story.

Fun Facts about the Movie
A Dog's Way Home

★ Shelby was not the only movie dog who performed as Bella. There were actually three dogs who acted out Bella's story. One of them, Luke, is owned by Shelby's trainer, Teresa. Luke and Shelby look almost identical. When Bruce first saw Shelby at the shelter, he had no idea that she would shortly be living with a friend who looked so much like her! Luke did most of the scenes that called for Bella to growl or fight. (Shelby's sweet nature means she isn't much good at acting ferocious.) Since the plan called for three dogs to play the part of Bella, Teresa searched far and wide to find a third dog, Amber, who looks so much like Luke and Shelby that people cannot always tell them apart.

★ A Dog's Way Home was mostly filmed in British Columbia, Canada. Shelby, her trainers, the actors, and the camera crew spent several weeks tromping over the Rocky Mountains to get the shots they needed for the movie.

★ Scenes in a movie are often filmed out of order. The avalanche scene, which comes at the end of *Shelby's Story,* actually occurs fairly early in the movie. Other scenes, such as Shelby's encounters with her cougar companion, Big Kitten, come later. After the scenes are filmed, they are arranged in order so that the story makes sense.

★ The people who work on movies are very careful to ensure the safety of all animals. On the set of *A Dog's Way Home,* Teresa and other trainers kept a close eye on Shelby and the other dogs at all times. Other people on the set work for an organization whose entire job is making sure that animals in films are well treated. Sometimes shooting was stopped so that the dogs could rest and get warm or cool off. And never once did the dogs mingle with actual coyotes or cougars, even though in the movie it looks like Bella is nose-to-nose with these animals!

★ It is unusual for a book's author (in this case, W. Bruce Cameron) to also be one of the screenwriters. He and his wife, Cathryn, are an accomplished writing team. Besides *A Dog's Way Home,* they were co-screenwriters on *A Dog's Purpose,* the upcoming *A Dog's Journey,* and two other movies: *Cook Off!* and *Muffin Top: A Love Story.* These last two movies were directed by Cathryn. Meanwhile, Bruce is hard at work writing more Puppy Tales, including *Toby's Story.*

Reading & Activity Guide to
Shelby's Story:
A Dog's Way Home Tale
By W. Bruce Cameron

Ages 8–12; Grades 3–7

A real-life dog named Shelby, who played the lead role of "Bella" in the movie version of the author's popular book *A Dog's Way Home,* inspired W. Bruce Cameron to write *Shelby's Story: A Dog's Way Home Tale.* In the humorous, candid voice of Shelby herself, *Shelby's Story: A Dog's Way Home Tale* gives the reader a dog's-eye view of an animal actor training, preparing for, and playing a lead role in a major motion picture. But before readers see Shelby balancing the challenges and perks of being a movie star, they learn the fictionalized Shelby's "back story." Readers follow Shelby's paw prints along her harsh, often unforgiving, path from hungry puppy of an indifferent owner; to scavenging stray; starving landfill stowaway; and, at last, a relieved, but puzzled, rescue shelter resident. Part Pit Bull, part Rottweiler, part mystery-breed, Shelby goes from life on the streets to life on the screen, when movie animal trainer Teresa adopts her. Shelby resembles Bella physically, but her story mirrors Bella's, too. Both dogs overcome obstacles, help people, and learn to let people help them. Bella and Shelby both find their way home, but also learn the true meaning of home. It's not just a place where you have what you need, but a place where you are *needed.* And the fictionalized

Shelby, who makes the incredible journey from rescue to red carpet, learns that "Bella" isn't her most important role. Shelby's most important role is being Teresa's dog!

(W. Bruce Cameron has written other dog tales, such as *Ellie's Story, Bailey's Story, Molly's Story, and Max's Story.* If you have had, or have, an opportunity to read them, you can discuss how the dogs and tales are similar and how they differ. It might also be interesting to check out, together with an older sibling or family member, the *A Dog's Way Home* novel and movie. Then you can discuss the connections and inspirations the *A Dog's Way Home* novel and movie, and *Shelby's Story: A Dog's Way Home Tale* share.)

Reading *Shelby's Story: A Dog's Way Home Tale* with Your Children

Pre-Reading Discussion Questions

1. Watching real-life dog actor Shelby in action making the movie version of his novel *A Dog's Way Home,* inspired W. Bruce Cameron to write *Shelby's Story.* Have you seen any movies where a dog was the main character? Which movies? How do you think the filmmakers got the dog to do certain things on command—like bark, run, jump, lie down, pick something up, or react to a person or situation in a particular way?

2. In *Shelby's Story: A Dog's Way Home Tale,* rescue dog Shelby is being trained to play the role of "Bella" for the film adaptation of *A Dog's Way Home.* Bella's often harrowing, but always heartfelt, journey back to the person who needs her, and the person she needs—no matter how many miles or obstacles stand between them—makes for a compelling story on the page or onscreen. Can you think of stories, or books, which had dogs as main characters? Would you like to see one of them made into a movie? Which one would you pick and why?

3. Street-toughened, but tender-hearted pup Shelby is the main character and narrator in *Shelby's Story: A Dog's Way Home Tale*, so readers have access to all her thoughts and feelings. Have you ever wondered what your own, or a friend's, dog was thinking or feeling? Do you think your dog, or pet, can tell how *you* are feeling? Why or why not? Do you feel like you can communicate with your dog or pet even if you can't have an actual conversation with an animal like you can with another person?

Post-Reading Discussion Questions

1. The whole story is told from Shelby the dog's point of view. Do you think having a dog telling the tale affects your reaction to the story? Do you think you would feel differently about the story if it were told from a human narrator's point of view? How are canine and human perspectives similar? How are they different?

2. During her puppyhood in Chapter 1, Shelby seems to enjoy the warmth and comfort of her canine family, but what impression do you get of her original human caretakers and circumstances from her description?

3. Since she doesn't know human language and labels for things, Shelby often observes objects with vivid, and often humorous, detail, guided by her sense of smell, taste, and touch. For example, in Chapter 1, she comes up with this description of dandelions: "They were fuzzy yellow circles attached to strong stems. They did not taste very good, but when I bit at them, they bobbed and danced on their stems, and that was almost like a game." Can you recall, or find, some of Shelby's other descriptions from the novel that you found particularly colorful or funny?

4. A recurring theme in Shelby's puppyhood is her intense and chronic hunger. Why do you think author W. Bruce Cameron chooses to have Shelby describe the hunger almost as if it as an animated thing separate from Shelby herself?

5. Shelby is conflicted between staying in the security and familiarity of her yard and exploring the world beyond the fence, with its potential for food and adventure. Have you ever been in a situation where you were torn between doing something that was familiar and trying something new? What does Shelby decide to do?

6. In Chapter 2, Shelby and her sister, Splotch, are scavenging for food. How do people's differing reactions to the stray pups reveal the great variety in human nature? Do you think Shelby makes the right choice to run away when the dogcatcher captures Splotch?

7. How does the man who works at the dump reinforce Shelby's distrust and fear of people? When Megan from the animal shelter rescues Shelby from the dump, what does Shelby observe about how different Megan's voice, behavior, and body language is from other humans Shelby has encountered?

8. In Chapter 5, Bruce, Cathryn, and Teresa come to meet Shelby at the shelter. Who do Bruce and Cathryn think Shelby looks like? Why is this important? The "character" Bruce is actually author W. Bruce Cameron, who appears in the story because it is largely about his experiences with real-life animal actor Shelby. Throughout the story, Shelby makes funny comments about Bruce, including sarcastic comments and jokes at his expense. Does knowing that Bruce himself is actually writing those comments add to their humor?

9. Observing Shelby's confidence in, and affection for, Megan, animal trainer Teresa comments: "If Shelby can trust, if Shelby can love, then she can be trained." Why do you think Teresa needed to see these qualities in Shelby before she agreed to train her for the role of "Bella" in the movie *A Dog's Way Home*? Teresa brings Shelby home and Shelby meets Teresa's other dogs, Luke, Bode, Hercules, and Angel. Shelby is thrilled to be part of a "pack" again, but makes sure to use "good manners." For example, Shelby observes: "She jumped up to bark at me, and I let my ears droop to show her that I had not meant to be disrespectful." What do you learn about canine good manners (or "PETiquette") from Shelby's interactions with Teresa's dogs, and other dogs throughout the story?

10. Shelby learns that in addition to a new home, she has a new job called "Training." How does Teresa use treats, practice, and praise to teach Shelby commands like "Come," "Sit," "Stay," and "Go Mark"?

11. How does author W. Bruce Cameron cleverly use Shelby's canine perspective to deliver a humorous, but informative description of life on a movie set in Chapters 9 and 10? Why is "Go Mark" such a critical skill for a movie dog? How is Shelby's confusion about the term "Cut!" on the movie set a good illustration of how confusing and hard to decipher human behavior and language can be from an animal's perspective?

12. W. Bruce Cameron uses the dialogue between screenwriters Cathryn and Bruce to provide more information about some of the specifics of the filming process, which he can't logically weave in to Shelby's observations. What are some of the details you learn about filmmaking in general, and filming scenes for *A*

Dog's Way Home in particular, from the dialogue between these two characters?

13. Professionals like Teresa, April, and Brian, who work with Shelby and other dog actors in this story, are not just trainers, but also caretakers for their animals. What special gear and accommodations does Shelby receive on the set of *A Dog's Way Home*?

14. Shelby's bond with, and desire to please, Teresa is even more important than treats and training. How does Shelby's struggle with the pretend deer carcass in Chapter 11 confirm this? How does Teresa's handling of the aggressive Shaggy Male dog actor in Chapter 12 demonstrate that she fully reciprocates Shelby's love and concern?

15. Going to the red-carpet premiere of *A Dog's Way Home* is fun for Shelby, but the real cause of celebration for her is having "her own person" and a real home. How has Shelby's definition of home changed over the course of the story?

Post-Reading Activities
Take the story from the page to the pavement with these fun and inspiring activities for the dog lovers in your family.

1. TREATS, CAMERA, ACTION! In *Shelby's Story: A Dog's Way Home Tale*, animal trainer Teresa adopts Shelby from a shelter, to play the role of "Bella," the canine main character in the movie made from W. Bruce Cameron's book *A Dog's Way Home*. Invite your child to work with you and other family members and friends to make a mini-movie with your dog, or a friend's dog, as the main character. Will it be a mystery (*The Case of the Missing Shoe*)? Or maybe a comedy (*The Dog Ate My Homework*)? Together, you'll need to develop a short script, which includes: a list of characters (animal and human); the dialogue·that will be spoken by the human actors in the movie; the actions or behaviors the dog or other animal actors will need to perform; and descriptions of the locations where the action and dialogue unfold. Using training techniques and methods described in *Shelby's Story: A Dog's Way Home Tale*, try to train your dog to perform any additional tricks, stunts, or actions your script requires. As you saw from the book, making a movie involves a lot of people. You might want to assign roles to friends and family participating in the mini-movie project, such as: scriptwriter, actors, animal trainer, camera operator (using or borrowing a phone or other device with audio/video capability), and director. Make sure your child has your, or appropriate adult, supervision and permission for all activities and locations, and that all aspects are safe and reasonable for human and animal actors! Consider organizing a Red CarPET premiere party modeled after the one Shelby gets to attend. Invite friends and family to a screening of the mini-movie. You might invite guests to bring dog food, treats, blankets, toys, collars, leashes, or other gear, as (optional) "admission" to the premiere. You can donate those supplies to a local animal shelter, like the one that rescued and housed Shelby before she became a movie star!

2. PURPOSEFUL (aka PUR-PAWS-FULL) PROJECTS

In *Shelby's Story, A Dog's Way Home Tale*, Shelby liked having a clear mission, especially if it meant helping Teresa. Brainstorm ideas with your child about ways that he or she, together with their dog or a friend's dog, can help your household or community. For example, can your child invite a family member who has been trying to get more exercise, or reduce stress, to go on a regular dog walk? Do friends or neighbors have dogs that have to be crated for long periods of time due to work schedules, or other activities away from their home? Can you help your child offer, and make arrangements, to bring the dogs in need of attention to a dog park or other dog-friendly area where your child and dog can help provide those dogs with extra attention and activity while their owners are unavailable? Or perhaps you can help your child reach out to dog owners who are more elderly, who could use some help and company as they care for, and exercise, their dogs.

3. WAGGING TAILS AND WRITING TALES! Author W. Bruce Cameron was inspired to write *Shelby's Story: A Dog's Way Home Tale* because of his firsthand experience with dog actor Shelby, who played the determined dog "Bella," in the movie being made of his book, *A Dog's Way Home*. Ask your child if they can think of an animal-related experience or observation which might spark their interest and imagination like meeting dog actor Shelby inspired Mr. Cameron. Invite your child to write a short story based on that experience. In *Shelby's Story: A Dog's Way Home*, Mr. Cameron blends what he learned and observed with fictionalized material. Encourage your child to blend imagination and information in their story, too.

Reading *Shelby's Story: A Dog's Way Home Tale* in Your Classroom

These Common Core-aligned writing activities may be used in conjunction with the pre- and post-reading discussion questions above.

1. Point of View: When animal trainer Teresa adopts Shelby, she adds a new member to the diverse canine crew, which already shares her home. Since the novel is written from Shelby's point of view, we learn how Shelby feels about "moving in," but what do Teresa's dogs (Luke, Bode, Hercules, and Angel) think of the newcomer? How might each of them describe Shelby's appearance, attitude, relationship with Teresa, and how the arrival of a new dog affects the dynamics of their "pack"? Pick one of Teresa's other dogs and write 2–3 paragraphs from that dog's point of view. Draw on details from the novel, and the example of the unique voice W. Bruce Cameron created for Shelby, to help you give your chosen dog an engaging, authentic point of view.

2. Home Is More Than Just a (Dog) House: In a one-page essay, discuss how the concept of finding your true home is important to both the plot and theme of *Shelby's Story*. Using examples and details from the text, recall the different "homes" Shelby experiences (including her puppy home with an apathetic owner; scavenging on the streets with her sister, Splotch; life at the landfill; adapting to shelter living; trying to make sense of pens and hotels in transit to Teresa's; and, at last, finding a real home with Teresa and her dogs. Explore how Shelby's definition of home evolves throughout the story, and how she comes to realize that "home" can and should be so much more than just a roof over your head.

3. Text Type: Opinion Piece. Shelby is part Pit Bull, part Rottweiler, and part "something else." Pit Bulls have gotten a lot of "bad press" for being a dangerous and aggressive breed. Shelby, like her screen persona "Bella," offers a positive portrayal of a dog from Pit heritage, but dogs that are full, or part, Pit Bull often have a negative reputation. In your opinion, is it possible for Pit Bull owners and breeders to improve the breed's image? Why or why not? In a one-page essay, articulate and support your opinion. If you do think it is possible to wage a successful "public relations campaign" for the breed, include suggestions for what Pit Bull fans might do to encourage others to reconsider their view of the breed.

4. Text Type: Narrative. In *Shelby's Story,* the reader learns from Shelby's perspective how it felt to be a stray that gets rescued, adopted, and eventually trained to be a dog actor with a starring role in a movie. How might the story be different if animal trainer Teresa was the narrator? In the character of Teresa, describe what it was like to meet Shelby, and welcome her to your life and home (with four dogs already in residence) and prepare her to take on the role of "Bella". What were the biggest challenges and rewards during the training and filming process? Were you confident that you could turn a stray into a star? Did Bella teach *you* anything new, professionally or personally?

5. Research & Present: WORKING LIKE A DOG: ANIMAL WELFARE IN THE ENTERTAINMENT INDUSTRY. Do online and library research to learn how animals are cast, trained, and treated in television, movies, and commercials. What are the laws and logistics around animal actors? How have issues and concerns been addressed, and improvements made, to ensure humane treatment of animals in entertainment? What positions and policies have animal-welfare organizations developed to protect animal rights and well being? (HINT: Check out organizations such as the AHA, American Humane Association.) How and why do production companies earn the credit that "no animal was harmed" (in the making of this film/show/commercial)? Create a PowerPoint or other multimedia-style presentation to share your findings with classmates.

6. Research & Present: PAWS FOR APPLAUSE: THE JOB OF AN ANIMAL TRAINER. In *Shelby's Story*, Teresa, April, and Brian are animal trainers. Being an animal trainer is a demanding, if rewarding, job. Often, the trainers are also the animals' owners, so they are caretakers as well as trainers. In small groups, use your local library and online resources to learn about different aspects of this unique job. What education, training, and experience are required? What kinds of opportunities and salaries are there in this field? Who are some of the most respected trainers in the industry, and what are some of the popular films or television shows in which their animals have been used? How might the increased use of digital animation instead of live animal actors affect the future of this job? Work collaboratively to organize your research findings in an oral presentation, supported by colorful visual and written aids (such as pamphlets and posters), to deliver to classmates. Each student should also write a summary of what they learned about the work of movie animal trainers.

Supports English Language Arts Common Core Writing Standards: W.3.1, 3.2, 3.3, 3.7; W.4.1, 4.2, 4.3, 4.7; W.5.1, 5.2, 5.3, 5.7; W.6.2, 6.3, 6.7; W.7.2, 7.3, 7.7

Introducing

BruceCameronKidsBooks.com

the brand-new hub for
W. Bruce Cameron's
bestselling adventure tales

Check out fun videos and downloadable
activities paw-fect for the whole family!